No Longer Alone

Alone Trilogy
Book 3

Judith Bixby-Boling

To the Thursday Writers Critique Group

Thank you, Gloria Getman, Irene Morse, Shirley A. Blair Keller, Roger Boling, and Grace Dalton, for the many hours spent critiquing my work

Prologue

Captain Ian McClain stood before me on the train platform.

"I'm going to miss you. Priscilla Llewellyn." His voice was husky with emotion.

"Come with me," I implored for the hundredth time. "You have been invited to the wedding."

He moved his head from side to side. "I must get back to my ships. I've been away from them far too long. The *Emma* will leave tomorrow to take on cargo in New York. We'll likely be able to fill the hold before we reach Florida and turn towards Cuba. I was to be aboard the *Evangeline* when she took her first voyage around the Horn."

"I know. I am sorry." I dropped my gaze. "The *Evangeline* is a beautiful ship. I'm glad Elizabeth and I attended her launch. It was a very special day."

He placed his right index finger under my chin and lifted my head, forcing me to meet his gaze. "Come with me. You could disembark in Philadelphia, take trains to Gettysburg, and reboard the ship in Baltimore. Elizabeth would understand."

"We have had this conversation. I cannot live on a ship like your mother did. It is not in my nature, just as it is not in your nature, to live on land for more than a few months at a time. It's best we part now."

A train whistle sounded, and a conductor shouted, "All aboard."

"I must go." I stood on tip-toe to kiss Ian one last time.

"Write to me. I must know you are well."

"I shall. Now, go board the train."

He remained on the platform while I boarded and sat at a window.

We waved. I blew a kiss and watched him until the train pulled away. "I will miss you, Ian McClain," I whispered and closed my eyes. A lone tear found its way down my face.

Part 1
New Beginnings

Chapter 1

Gettysburg, Pennsylvania

It was afternoon when I stepped off the train from Hanover Junction. After arranging for my luggage to be delivered to Elizabeth Owens' home, I took a cab to the same destination.

Martha, Elizabeth's maid and cook, greeted me with squeals of joy, helped me out of my paletot, and showed me into the sitting room.

Elizabeth rose from a chair to hug me and took my hand to lead me to the sofa. "I'm so glad you're here," she said, settling on the sofa at an angle to more easily look at me.

"I am pleased to be here, too," I said, only slightly more restrained. "My baggage will be delivered this evening."

"I'll see to it," Martha volunteered with looks to her mistress and me.

"Thank you," I said, then returned my attention to my friend.

"So, how are the wedding plans?"

Elizabeth sobered, held up a hand, and began ticking off items on her fingers. "The church is reserved. Oliver and I have an appointment to meet with Pastor Johnson one last time before the wedding. The invitations have been sent. My dress is being made. I have a fitting in two weeks. Dinah and Lars are hosting the wedding breakfast. My parents are hosting the reception. Oliver is making reservations for our wedding trip." She settled her hand in her lap. "How are you? Are you recovered from your injury?"

"The doctor said the arm and shoulder are healed."

"When will Captain McClain be arriving?"

I did not answer immediately. "He sends his best wishes for a happy marriage. He will not be attending your wedding. He is aboard the *Emma*, heading down the east coast, and will ultimately sail to Cuba."

"Has he fully recovered from the fever?"

"Yes. The sea air at Ipswich and his mother's fine cooking were the healing balm he required."

"Are you making your own wedding plans?" There was an expectancy in her voice.

I shook my head. "There is no betrothal."

"Why not?"

"Because although we share affection for one another, we would not be happy in a marriage. He lives on the sea, moving from place to place and never settling anywhere. I prefer to live on land and remain in one place. One of us would always be miserable. We shall remain friends."

"I'm so sorry." She turned to place her feet on the floor when Martha came in with a tea tray.

The maid moved so quietly, I was unaware she had gone to the kitchen.

Elizabeth poured out and offered a plate of freshly baked cookies.

"Will you and Oliver live here after you're married?"

"No. I'll rent it out. Oliver bought a house for us. I must go over to let a workman in. Come with me, and I'll give you the penny tour."

"I would like that." I bit into a still-warm cookie. "This is delicious."

We ate, drank tea, and talked for another hour, then walked the four blocks to the house Oliver had purchased.

"My word. It is large," I proclaimed.

"I agree. I wanted something smaller, but this was his choice. He says we'll grow into it."

"You could have ten children and still have unused space," I observed.

Elizabeth laughed. "Close, but not quite." She unlocked the door when a wagon pulled up in front of the house, driven by a man in work clothes.

"Mrs. Finch?" he asked.

"Not yet, but soon." Elizabeth turned towards the man. "For the next month, I'm Mrs. Owens."

"Begging your pardon, ma'am. Mr. Finch hired me to repair the banister on the staircase."

"Nice to meet you." Elizabeth opened the door and stepped aside, allowing the man and me to enter.

The house was every bit as grand on the inside, and the odor of fresh paint hung in the air.

"Let's open some windows," Elizabeth suggested. "That odor is vile."

"It always reminds me of skunks," I observed, walking to a window, unlocking and opening it.

"Yes, exactly," Elizabeth said. She then turned to the workman at the foot of the stairs. "I'm sorry I don't recall your name."

"I'm Chester Woodhouse."

"How long do you think you'll need to repair the banisters?"

"It will take a couple of days. I'll finish up today around four. I want to finish for the day before I lose daylight."

"I'll be back before four to close the windows and lock up. I'll come back around seven tomorrow morning to let you in."

"That will be fine, Mrs. Owens."

With her business concluded, Elizabeth and I explored the house before returning to her home.

Before Elizabeth and I sat down for supper, I asked whether Oliver would join us.

"No. He's out of town until the twenty-third."

Delighted to have my friend to myself, I chose not to ask why he was gone.

"So, what do you want to do while you're here?" Elizabeth asked.

"I would love to visit with your mother and Dinah."

"Dinah invited us to dinner tomorrow afternoon," Elizabeth shared.

"Wonderful. I enjoy her company and adore Hetty and Caleb."

"You won't recognize either of them. They've both grown so much. Hetty will be five years old in a few months, and Caleb walks and says a few words."

"I always smile when I recall Hetty's attempts to say 'Lewellyn.'"

"It amused me, too. But Dinah was embarrassed by it. She taught Hetty to say it properly."

"That saddens me. It's not an easy name to pronounce when someone is so young."

Changing the subject, Elizabeth said, "I have been thinking about going to the farm next week. The ground hasn't thawed sufficiently, but Papa is preparing for spring planting.

"Mama has been sewing a new dress for the wedding. Papa refused to allow her to go to a dressmaker."

"Will you go for the day?"

"No, I'll stay the week. I won't be able to visit as frequently after the wedding."

"No, I suppose not. At least, not alone," I acknowledged.

We ate quietly for a few moments.

"You have not mentioned your other sister. How are Ruth and Wolfgang?" I asked.

"All right, I suppose. I seldom see them. Ruth and I prefer it that way. Mama told me they will be attending the wedding." Elizabeth finished eating the food on her plate. "Are you ready for dessert? Or would you rather wait a bit?"

I pushed back from the table. "I would prefer to wait if you do not mind."

"That's my preference, too. Let's go back to the sitting room." She stood and led the way.

Once settled with our feet tucked under ourselves, I asked, "How is Gertrude?"

Elizabeth stared at the fire in the fireplace. "We've not spoken in a fortnight."

Astonishment washed over me. My mouth gaped open as I took in the sour expression on my friend's face. "What happened?"

"She's taken a dislike to Oliver. The dislike is mutual." She stood to put another log on the fire, then resettled herself before continuing. "When Oliver tried to forbid me from associating with her, she declared our business arrangement at an end unless I broke it off with Oliver."

"I do not see either of those options sitting well with you."

"I told Oliver he wasn't yet my husband and had no authority to determine with whom I associated. Then, I told Gertrude she could not select whom I chose to marry. We've not spoken since. It breaks my heart to no longer work with the widows. We've made such progress." She sniffed and brushed away tears from under her eyes.

Chapter 2

15 March 1867

Elizabeth and I arrived at the Hoffman home at half past twelve.

Hetty opened the door and threw her arms around my waist. "Oh, Miss Llewellyn, I'm so happy to see you," the little girl declared as she spoke into the skirt of my dress. "Hello, Aunt Beth."

"I am delighted to be with you again, Hetty," I replied.

She released her grasp and turned to shout, "Mama, Aunt Beth, and Miss Loolyn are here."

I smiled at the child's mispronunciation of my name.

"Hetty," Elizabeth began.

"No, please, do not correct her," I begged. "I find it endearing. I would love her to call me 'Miss Loolyn' forever."

"Really?" Elizabeth asked. "She worked very hard to learn to say 'Llewellyn.'"

"I'm sure she did. But, please don't make her change."

Dinah came into the foyer. "Hetty, it's time you went upstairs. You don't have to sleep, but you must rest." She turned to her guests. "Welcome back, Priscilla. Good afternoon, Beth. Do you mind if we eat in the kitchen? I'm baking pies for the grocers."

"How are Mr. and Mrs. Grimes?" I asked.

"They're both well. My pastries are selling faster than I can bake. I'm baking for them three days a week and still cannot keep up with the demand."

"How do you find the time to do everything?" Elizabeth

asked. "Your home is immaculate. Your children are well-behaved and adorably dressed. You serve on the altar guild at Christ Church. You've always got something on your sewing machine. And you bake pastries three days a week to sell at the grocer's. When do you sleep?"

"'Ask me no questions, and I'll tell you no lies,'" Dinah quoted the ancient proverb with an impish grin. "How are you, Priscilla? Beth told me you suffered an injury. Why would anyone do that?"

"Josiah Pennyman, the man in Texas to whom I was briefly betrothed, owed a debt to a man named Percival Templeton. Percival died before it was paid. Josiah passed away a short time later, still owing the debt. Percival's twin brother, Augustus, thought it was incumbent upon me to satisfy the debt. When I refused, he shot me with a pistol."

"I seem to recall Beth telling me you were betrothed to a cattleman."

"Josiah Pennyman could be quite charming when the occasion called for it. He was self-centered and cruel. I consider myself fortunate to have seen his true nature before we were wed."

"Let's talk of more pleasant things," Elizabeth suggested. "Did you know Priscilla will interview for a teaching position in Philadelphia? She and Agatha Bentley could be teaching at the same school.

"Agatha and you have been friends forever, Beth." Dinah served our meal from the stove. "We've corresponded for some time, though I've not heard from her recently."

"We were almost inseparable before I married Horace. Agatha teaches geography at Girls' High and Normal School in Philadelphia," Elizabeth said.

"It's the first public girls' school in Pennsylvania and accepts students from all walks of life at no direct cost to their families. The girls want to be there," I explained. "If the girls finish high school and continue with the normal school, they graduate as qualified teachers."

"I'd no idea anything like that existed," Dinah marveled.

Agatha wrote to tell me the French teacher will be married in June, and the school board is advertising for a replacement."

"Oh, I almost forgot. I received a note from Gertrude Schmidt yesterday," Dinah informed us. "Weren't you friends with her as well, Beth?"

"We were at school together, but we weren't friends. I didn't become friends with her until I returned to Gettysburg last year. She approached me about working with the war widows. Why would she be writing to you?" Elizabeth asked.

"I'm uncertain. She asked to meet with me. I told her I accept visitors on Wednesday afternoons."

"Perhaps she wants to speak with you about her work," I suggested.

"I sincerely doubt that," Elizabeth said. "She probably wants to talk about Oliver."

"I know she and Oliver don't get along," Dinah observed.

"That's an understatement. She is openly hostile towards him. I doubt she'll come to the wedding." There was bitterness in Elizabeth's words.

"Whatever the reason, I'll likely know tomorrow." Dinah ate the last of the food on her plate and went to take two pies out of the oven.

The three women lingered over tea and apple pie, with Dinah shifting baked and unbaked pies to and from the oven.

"Are you certain we cannot help clear up?" I asked as we prepared to leave.

"I'm positive," Dinah assured me. "I've my little helper. Hetty and I will manage quite nicely." She followed her sister and me through the hallway to the foyer. "How long will you stay in Gettysburg?"

"I must leave on the fifteenth of April," I informed her. "My interview is on the sixteenth.

"I hope to see you again while you're here."

"I'm certain you will. Good afternoon, Dinah. Thank you for a lovely dinner."

Elizabeth hugged her sister. "We're going to the farm next week. We'll see you when we return to Gettysburg."

Dinah stood at the door as we went down the walkway to the street, then closed it.

Chapter 3

I sat beside Elizabeth as she drove the buggy to her parents' farm.

"This buggy is much nicer than the carriages you have previously rented," I observed.

"I bought it last autumn. It's more convenient, though also a little more costly. The horse came from the farm. I board Buttercup at the livery stable and pay a fee to store the buggy there, too."

"I can see the wisdom in purchasing it. Papa bought one for me shortly after the war was declared. He complained it gave me too much independence. But I am certain his farm hands were relieved when they no longer had to drive me to Norwich several times a week."

"Oliver was against it at first, though I never learned why. Papa talked him round, though."

"Are your father and Oliver close?"

Elizabeth negotiated a turn before replying, "They appear to have a great deal in common—more so than Papa has with either of my brothers-in-law."

I pondered this piece of information. *Is their common goal to gain access to Elizabeth's bank accounts?* I kept the thought to myself.

We arrived at the farm before dinner and received warm greetings from Karl and Ada.

"Put your things upstairs," Ada instructed. "Priscilla, you're in Dinah's room. Dinner is almost ready."

"We'll be right down," Elizabeth promised as we went upstairs.

"How long do you girls plan to stay?" Ada asked as she served a savory stew and cornbread with pots of butter and honey.

"May we stay until Friday?" Elizabeth asked. "Oliver is out of town, and I have nothing pressing until Tuesday next week."

"What is so important about Tuesday of next week?" Karl asked.

"I have a dress fitting," she replied. "It will be the first time I'll see my wedding dress."

Ada's expression softened. "I'm sure it's lovely. What color did you decide on?"

"It's a light pink silk."

"Sounds expensive," Karl grumbled.

"Then you should be thankful you're not paying for it," Ada retorted. "It's her wedding dress."

"She already has a wedding dress."

"That one is white and inappropriate for a second marriage," Elizabeth explained. "I wouldn't think you or Oliver would want me to cause a scandal."

"Hmph," Karl replied. "No, I suppose not."

"Papa, it will be a modest wedding. I'm not asking anything of you except that you attend."

Karl ate his meal without further comment.

Elizabeth and I gathered eggs every morning and helped prepare meals. We took long walks on the farm and rode horses to visit neighbors on adjoining farms. We sat in the sitting room, knitting and mending, while Ada finished sewing the dress she would wear to the wedding.

On Tuesday afternoon, I went into the kitchen to bring in the pot of tea that had been brewing for some minutes. Karl was there, drinking coffee and looking at a large sheet of paper spread out on the table.

I glanced at the paper and instantly recognized it. "My father planned his crop planting using that same method," I said.

"What did he plant?" Karl asked.

"Alfalfa and grains for the horses, and vegetables. He sold the vegetables in town."

"Did he keep some back for your kitchen?"

"No, we had a separate kitchen garden with a greater variety than we grew to sell."

"Your mother must have enjoyed that."

"My mother died when I was five days old. Our cook, Mrs. Farnsworth, reaped the benefits of the kitchen garden."

"I'm sorry. I didn't know."

I nodded, acknowledging the kindness. "What are you going to plant this year?" I asked, genuinely interested.

Karl pointed to a large field. "Corn will go here." He moved his hand to the adjacent plot. "Wheat here." He then indicated a small plot nearer the house. "Ada doesn't know yet, but I'll plant flowers here."

I smiled. "I will keep your secret. Mrs. Baumann will love it."

"She's never asked but has made pointed comments about other gardens."

"Why are you so harsh with Elizabeth?" The question escaped before I could stop it.

He looked at me, his expression a combination of surprise and annoyance.

"I'm sorry. I should not pry."

"Elizabeth is strong-willed and has an independent streak a mile wide. She needs to know her place. Oliver will see to that."

I was struck speechless and stared at him with what I am certain was a shocked and pained expression. I picked up the teapot and left without comment.

Later that day, Elizabeth and I were walking in a pasture, watching horses chase one another and occasionally coming to us.

I was stroking Buttercup's nose, deep in thought.

"A penny for your thoughts," Elizabeth said, coming up beside me and touching the horse's neck.

"I was thinking about my horse in Norwich. Her name is Gwen. She's saddle broken but also pulled my buggy." I glanced sideways at Elizabeth. "Buttercup reminds me of her."

"She's a sweetheart." Elizabeth moved around behind me, allowing the horse to see her. "I forgot you lived on a farm."

"Papa bred horses and sheep. The horses were frequently cross-trained like Gwen and sold to whoever needed a mount or carriage horse. He provided horses to the Connecticut Volunteer Calvary and Infantry during the war. Two or three times a year, the farmhands would herd most of the sheep to Norwich and put them on a train. I have no idea where they went." I patted Buttercup's neck and moved away from the palomino.

Friday dawned all too soon. Elizabeth and I removed the linen from our beds and packed our bags before gathering eggs and setting the table for breakfast.

There was little conversation until Karl rose from the table. "You girls take care driving back to town," he said as he moved towards the hallway leading to the farm office.

"We will, Papa." Elizabeth went to him and kissed his cheek. "We'll see you at church on Sunday."

"Thank you, Mr. Baumann. I enjoyed my visit. I wish you a good growing season."

"Goodbye, Miss Llewellyn." Karl disappeared down the hall, I began clearing the table.

"Stop that now," Ada commanded. "The dishes will wait. Let's sit and have another cup of tea."

Elizabeth and I exchanged looks and dutifully sat.

"I so enjoy your visits. I suspect there won't be many after you're married."

"I'm certain Oliver wouldn't mind if I came to stay a day or two now and again," Elizabeth speculated.

"He will likely expect you to stay home with him," I pointed out.

"He'll have to understand my family is important to me," Elizabeth replied.

"Oliver may not be that understanding," Ada advised, the teacup halfway to her mouth. "Perhaps you should speak with him about it before the wedding."

Elizabeth glared at us. "He'll understand." She stood and left the kitchen.

Ada and I listened to her footfalls on the stairs.

"I do not believe Oliver Finch is the understanding type," I said quietly, taking the dirty dishes to the sink.

"Neither do I." Ada poured hot water from the kettle into the dishpan.

Elizabeth and I left before dinner and rode in silence for nearly half an hour.

"I am sorry about the conversation earlier," I offered.

"I am, too," she said, keeping her eyes on the horse and road. "I'm sometimes over-sensitive about Oliver. People seem to think he is controlling, but he's not—at least not with me."

"I pray he allows you a modicum of independence."

"He will."

Chapter 4

14 April 1867
Gettysburg, Pennsylvania

I received a warm greeting from Agatha Bentley in the narthex of Christ Church. We had corresponded but hadn't been together since I left Philadelphia with Elizabeth the previous autumn.

An usher seated us in the pew behind Elizabeth's parents. Gertrude Schmidt was already seated on the aisle. Agatha sat to her left. I filed into the pew after Agatha.

I nodded to Gertrude. She managed an insincere smile and turned her attention to the altar where Oliver Finch and Lars Hoffman, Dinah's husband, stood to the minister's left.

Elizabeth walked down the sanctuary's center aisle alone to meet her betrothed at the altar. She was a vision in her pale pink silk dress, with matching hat and gloves. She carried her white leather-covered Bible but no flowers. Dinah was her matron of honor.

The bride and groom spoke their vows loudly and clearly.

Afterward, family and friends formed a procession from Christ Church to the home of Lars and Dinah Hoffman to enjoy a quiet reception.

Chapter 5

15 April 1867
Philadelphia, Pennsylvania

Agatha and I left Gettysburg on the Monday morning train to Hanover Junction and traveled by two more trains to Philadelphia.

Agatha took a cab to Mrs. Peele's boardinghouse. Another cab wended its way to La Pierre House, where I secured a room.

I went directly to the dining room to take my supper alone and dropped into bed before 9 pm.

Chapter 6

16 April 1867
Girls' High and Normal School
Philadelphia, Pennsylvania

"Our curriculum is confined to academic subjects to train future teachers," Mr. George Fetter informed me. He was a middle-aged man of average build and balding. Miss Tremblay, our French teacher, is to be married during the summer and will not be returning. How did you come to know French?"

"My father hired tutors to ensure I could fluently speak, read, and write the language," I informed him, allowing this information to settle.

"Since you have no experience, Miss Llewellyn, we must devise a method of evaluating your ability to teach French. Would you be amenable to our observing you in the classroom?"

I closed my eyes, my thoughts racing. When I opened them, I nodded. "Yes. I would be delighted to have that opportunity."

He rose from his chair and walked around his desk. "We shall speak with Miss Tremblay. She will provide you with her lesson plans for Thursday, and you will teach all her classes."

I worked to contain my excitement.

Mademoiselle Tremblay was a thin woman with severe features. Her voice had a nasal quality. She was pleased to learn of my interest in teaching French. We conversed briefly in the language before she quickly reviewed the lessons she planned for Thursday. She provided copies of the materials I was to teach.

Mr. Fetter and I returned downstairs.

"Report to me no later than half past seven on Thursday morning. Classes start at eight," the principal informed me.

"Thank you for this opportunity. I shall see you Thursday morning," I said as I left the school.

I strolled through an older neighborhood with budding trees and greening lawns. Few people were in their yards at this time of the day. Turning a corner, I quickened my pace and soon stood on the stoop of Mrs. Peele's boardinghouse and knocked on the door.

"Miss Llewellyn, how lovely to see you again," Mrs. Naomi Peele smiled and stepped aside to allow me entry into her home. "When did you return to Philadelphia?"

"Good afternoon, Mrs. Peele. I arrived yesterday evening." I stepped into the foyer and followed the landlady into the drawing room, where we sat across from one another. "Would you, perchance, have a room for let?"

"Does that man continue to stalk you?" A wary expression crossed Mrs. Peele's countenance.

"No. Mr. Andrew Payne of the Pinkerton Detective Agency has removed himself to another state. The authorities have properly dealt with the people who hired him and who wished to harm Mrs. Owens and me."

"Praise the Lord. That is a relief." Mrs. Peele glanced heavenward. "I shall let you have a room on the second floor facing the back garden at the same rate I previously charged. I caution you, should there be any problems, you shall leave and forfeit your rent."

"Thank you, Mrs. Peele. I can assure you there is no one looking for me." I opened my reticle and extracted my purse. I handed her several coins. "That will cover this month and next month."

"That's not necessary. One week's rent will suffice."

"I hope paying for two months eases your mind that I shall not leave Philadelphia in the immediate future."

Her gaze moved from the coins in her hand to my face. "Thank you. When may I expect you to take up residency?"

"Would it be convenient to have my things delivered tomorrow morning?"

"That will be fine. I'll have one of my girls refresh the room and put linen on the bed."

"I've taken enough of your time. I'll go now and return tomorrow morning."

We stood and walked towards the door.

"Please come back this evening for supper. You will be able to meet the other boarders."

"Thank you, Mrs. Peele. I would like that very much. Shall I return around six?"

"That would be fine. I look forward to seeing you this evening, Miss Llewellyn."

I sat next to Agatha at supper, renewed my acquaintance with Miss Beulah Snodgrass, and met a new lodger, Miss Calah Sheftall.

Beulah was short and plump. I didn't recall her neglecting her appearance, but on this evening, her dress was soiled and wrinkled, and her hair was unkempt. *I wonder why she doesn't pay more attention to her appearance.*

Miss Sheftall was the picture of austerity in her dark blue dress, and her brown hair pulled back into a tight bun at the base of her neck.

Afterward, Agatha and I talked in her room.

"I recall Miss Snodgrass living here, but I don't know anything about her," I confessed.

"I don't know her well, either. She keeps herself to herself. I believe she works as a cleaner at a hospital."

"That would explain her disheveled appearance," I observed.

"I'm not sorry Miss Adams and Miss Crane weren't at supper. Miss Adams tends to be mean-spirited and gossipy. I suppose that's what happens to spinsters," Agatha lamented.

I laughed. "You know, at the ripe old age of twenty-three, we are both considered spinsters, don't you? I hope we're not considered 'gossipy.'" I looked at the watch attached to my dress. "I should return to the hotel and let you get some sleep."

"Slumber shall have to wait. I have papers to mark." Agatha moved to the small table where a short stack of papers sat. "I gave a test today, and the girls will expect it to be returned tomorrow."

"No peace for the wicked," I teased as I approached the door. "I'm returning to the hotel to review Mademoiselle Tremblay's lesson plans." I picked up my reticule and pulled on my gloves. "It is lovely to be with you again."

"It will be nice to have you under this roof once more. I'll pray you are offered the teaching position. Good evening, Priscilla."

I went downstairs, thanked Mrs. Peele again for a lovely supper, and left. As luck would have it, two women were alighting a cab as I walked towards the street. I briefly spoke with the driver and entered the cab for the ride to the hotel.

Chapter 7

17 April 1867
Mrs. Peele's Boardinghouse

After breaking my fast, I checked out of La Pierre House and went to Mrs. Peele's boardinghouse. I spent the morning unpacking and settling into the charming room on the second floor with a view of the back garden.

Two older women were seated at the table when I went down for dinner. "I'm Miss Priscilla Llewellyn. I moved in this morning."

"I'm Miss Barbara Adams," replied a woman with graying hair. She indicated the white-haired woman sitting to her left. "This is Miss Daphne Crane. Your departure last autumn was fortuitous for us. We called on Mrs. Peele and were able to take up residency the day after you and Mrs. Owens left her."

I felt no compunction to explain our hasty departure to these women.

We three sat with our hands in our laps and our gazes on our empty plates while Mrs. Peele's daughters placed bowls and a platter of cold meat on the table.

I took a deep breath and picked up a bowl of green beans. Having placed a generous serving on my plate, I handed the bowl to Miss Crane, then picked up the basket of biscuits, took two, and passed it along.

After dinner, I returned to my room with a cup of tea and a slice of cherry pie. I sat at the table and spent the entire afternoon continuing to familiarize myself with Mademoiselle Tremblay's plans and making notes for the lessons I would be teaching the next day.

.

Chapter 8

18 April 1867
Girls' High and Normal School

Agatha and I walked to the school, where Mr. Fetter met me in the reception hall. Agatha wished me luck and made her way to her classroom. The principal escorted me to Miss Tremblay's.

I greeted the French teacher, removed my hat and gloves, and hung up my shawl. I then arranged the materials for each class with my notes on the teacher's desk and wrote my name and several simple sentences in French on the chalkboard.

Girls filed into the room, whispering and glancing at me. I recalled my days at school in Norwich when we faced a new teacher and smiled knowingly. At eight o'clock, I stepped up to the desk and introduced myself. After taking the roll and marking students present or absent, I began the lesson.

Mr. Fetter and Miss Tremblay sat in the back of the room and watched intently.

Miss Tremblay and I talked about the lessons I taught that morning and the students in her classes as we ate dinner in the faculty dining room. After a brief trip to the necessary, we returned to the classroom, ready for the afternoon classes.

"You have done very well," Miss Tremblay praised as we prepared to leave at the end of the school day. "You are an excellent teacher."

"Thank you. The girls were very kind and receptive to the

lessons. They appeared eager to learn."

"It's Esme, please," she said. "I shall submit a written recommendation to the school board. I expect you'll receive their decision soon."

"My name is Priscilla," I replied. "I am grateful for this opportunity, Esme." I glanced around the room for Mr. Fetter.

"Mr. Fetter left at the end of class. He appeared to be pleased with your performance."

As we reached the bottom of the stairs, she held out her hand. "Good day, Priscilla. I'm certain we'll meet again."

"Good afternoon, Esme. I pray we shall."

I met Agatha outside, and we walked to the rooming house together.

"Some of the girls you taught were talking about you when they came to my room. They loved how you insisted they speak only French in class, even in the first years."

I felt a warm glow. "That's wonderful to hear. The girls were very attentive and polite. I thought it was perhaps because Miss Tremblay and Mr. Fetter were in the back of the room."

Agatha giggled. "That may have been part of it. But they were genuinely excited about the lessons today. Some of them were still speaking French when they came into my room. I don't speak the language well, but I understood enough to know they enjoyed your class."

"We must pray the board is of the same mind."

After crossing a busy street, Agatha asked, "What made you decide to return to Philadelphia?"

"I want to do something useful. What is more useful than teaching young minds? It is fortuitous the school must hire a French teacher."

"The school term will end in June. Do you have plans for the summer?"

"I want to become better acquainted with Philadelphia. There are always books to be read, and I may be preparing lesson plans."

"I hope I'm not being presumptuous in wanting to join your exploration of the city. I'm ashamed to admit I've not visited many of the city's historic landmarks."

We stopped walking, and I took both her hands in mine. "We will have a most enjoyable summer. I know we will."

Agatha squeezed, then dropped my hands and turned into the path that led to the front door of the boardinghouse.

Chapter 9

2 July 1867
Philadelphia, Pennsylvania

The letter from Girls' High and Normal School arrived with the morning post. I broke the sealing wax on the envelope and lifted the flap. My hands shook as I released the single sheet of paper from its confines and unfurled it. The page fluttered with my shaking hands.

The Philadelphia Board of Education offered me a position as a French teacher at a salary of $30 a month.

A smile spread across my face as I read the missive. I sat heavily on the bed, still holding the letter. *They're actually going to pay me to teach!* Abruptly, I moved to the table and penned my acceptance.

I then wrote to Esme Tremblay, inviting her to tea at Mrs. Doyle's Tea Shop on a date convenient to her.

Donning a hat and gloves, I placed the two envelopes in my shopping basket and walked to the post office before seeking the dressmaker Mrs. Peele had recommended.

I returned to the boardinghouse in time for dinner. After divesting myself of my shopping basket, hat, and gloves, I took my place at the dining table.

"Good afternoon, Miss Llewellyn," Calah Sheftall greeted with her Southern lilt. "How are you this fine day?" She wore a simple gray work dress. Smudges of flour on her forehead and the sleeves of her dress were testament that she had been baking. The fragrance of baking bread wafting from the kitchen confirmed that suspicion.

"Hello, Miss Sheftall. I'm well and in good spirits. I trust you are the same."

"I am."

We took our places at the dining table.

"What keeps you home today?" I asked.

"I do not teach on Fridays and Saturdays." She offered no further explanation. "How are you settling in?"

"Very well. It's not difficult when you have few possessions. Have you lived here for very long?"

"My family is from Georgia. We moved to New York in the early months of the war. I came to Philadelphia this past December to teach at the Girls' Hebrew School."

Mrs. Peele placed the meal on the table.

"I did not know there was a Hebrew school in Philadelphia."

"It opened last year. I started teaching there in January."

"What subject do you teach?"

"I teach Hebrew and mathematics. The girls' school is new, and there are few female teachers in the faith." Calah spooned vegetables on her plate and traded with me for the platter of cold beef.

We ate in silence for several minutes before Calah asked, "What brings you to Philadelphia, Miss Llewellyn?"

"A mutual friend and I came to Philadelphia last summer. She introduced me to Agatha, and we came to live here for a short time. Agatha and I corresponded after I left. She wrote to tell me the school was looking for a French teacher. I came in April to interview for the position. I received the offer for the position just this morning."

"Congratulations. French is a beautiful language and much easier to learn than Hebrew."

"I would suppose that to be true."

Miss Adams and Miss Crane slipped quietly into their chairs and filled their plates.

To alleviate the uncomfortable silence, I turned the conversation to historical sites in Philadelphia.

Chapter 10

As I came into the boardinghouse after having tea with Esme Tremblay Alden and going to the bookstore, I glanced at the letters on the table in the foyer and saw my name on two envelopes. I didn't recognize the penmanship on either, but knew the name in the return address of one. Wondering why Dinah Hoffman would write to me, I picked up both letters and went upstairs.

After dropping my satchel, hat, gloves, and reticule on the bed, I sat at the table and opened Dinah's letter.

Several sheets of paper were covered with the same scrawling writing as on the envelope, and I became increasingly agitated as I read. I must have emitted an excited utterance, as moments later, an urgent knocking on the door brought me out of the horror I had been reading.

"Priscilla, are you well?" Agatha asked from the hallway.

"Come in," I replied.

She opened the door and saw the crème-colored stationary in my hand. "Dinah wrote to both of us?" Agatha sat on the end of the bed. "I've heard of men institutionalizing their wives but never thought Oliver Finch would stoop so low as to send Elizabeth to an asylum."

"It is devastating. Did Dinah say anything in your letter about where she is?"

"No. I don't think she knows."

"I'm certain Mr. Baumann is in league with Oliver. He has

wanted to manage Elizabeth's affairs since she returned to Gettysburg. I do not know Lars well enough to know where he stands on the issue." I was reeling and trembled with fear and anger.

"What should we do?" Agatha asked.

"What can we do?" I retorted. "School will resume in two weeks. There are many asylums throughout Pennsylvania. Where would we begin to search for her?"

"I'll write to Dinah. Perhaps she has learned more since she wrote to us."

I did not respond. Agatha left my door open when she returned to her room.

Setting aside Dinah's letter, I took up the second envelope. The return address was an attorney in Gettysburg. I tore open the envelope and scanned the brief note.

Miss Llewellyn,
Mrs. Finch directed me to forward the enclosed letter to you in the event of a specific circumstance. Her fears have been realized. Her husband had her adjudged insane and committed to an asylum on the 15th of August.

D. McConaughy
Attorney-at-Law

Setting aside the note, I recognized Elizabeth's hand. Tears escaped down my cheeks and fell on the bodice of my dress.

Priscilla,

If you're reading this, Oliver has done his worst—to no avail. By now, he'll know I have placed all my holdings in several trusts with Mr. McConaughy as the trustee. Neither Oliver nor my father will be able to break them. Pray for me. I shall write if I am able.

Elizabeth

"Priscilla?" Calah said from the doorway.

I started at the sound of her voice. Setting the letter on the table, I looked up at her. "Good afternoon, Calah. What may I do for you?"

"This was just delivered." She held out a parcel.

"Thank you." I took it and held it on my lap as I broke the string around it.

"You look distressed. May I do anything to help you?"

"I just learned a friend is in a dire situation. I'm uncertain what to do."

"I won't pry. If you need to talk, I'm told I'm a good listener."

"What do you know about lunatic asylums?"

Her body jerked, her eyes widened, and her jaw tightened. "Is your friend in one of those places? I've heard they're unbearable."

"Agatha and I learned today that our friend's husband had her committed to one."

"That's awful. I've heard of women being sent to those places by their husbands because they argued or didn't have supper on the table on time."

"Do you know any lawyers?"

She smiled. "Three of my uncles are attorneys in Philadelphia."

"Agatha and I may want to speak with one of them."

"I'll be seeing them on Shabbat. I'll speak to them on Friday before sunset."

"Thank you, Calah."

She didn't respond but left me to open the parcel.

I unfolded the coarse brown paper to reveal five books I'd purchased that morning.

Chapter 11

16 September 1867
Philadelphia, Pennsylvania

With the start of the new school term, Agatha and I had little time to devote to searching for Elizabeth.

We wrote to Dinah and Mrs. Baumann, encouraging them and asking for any additional information they may have obtained to discover where Oliver had sent Elizabeth.

The boarders had gathered in the dining room for supper. Agatha and I were discussing a student who was struggling with her classes.

Calah passed behind our chairs and dropped a slip of paper on my plate.

I picked it up and unfolded it. Inside was the name and address of an attorney I presumed to be one of her uncles. I caught her attention and nodded my acknowledgment.

She smiled and placed her napkin on her lap.

Beulah Snodgrass shuffled in and sat next to Calah. I was struck by her more than usual disheveled appearance but said nothing.

"Good heavens, Miss Snodgrass, do you have no pride in your appearance?" Miss Adams sneered.

"I didn't have time to clean up before supper," Beulah replied, her voice quavering. "There was a problem on the ward, and I had to stay late."

Agatha and I looked at one another, then at Beulah.

"Where is it you are employed?" I asked.

"I work at Pennsylvania Hospital for the Insane," she replied without looking up from her lap.

"What do you do there?" Agatha enquired.

"I'm a cleaner on one of the women's wards. They're usually no bother, but one patient felt poorly. None of the nurses believed her, but then she was sick all over one of them, and I had to clean up the mess before I could leave for the day.

"The nurses didn't want to call for a doctor, but some of the other women started yelling and making a ruckus, so they finally sent for a doctor. By the time he got there, it was too late. The lady had died."

"Oh, that's horrible, Beulah." Calah touched her hand, which was red, raw, and puffy from cleaning six days a week.

"The doctor shouted at the nurses for not calling him sooner, and the nurses started striking the patients. I tried to stay out of the way but got knocked down, too."

"I've always heard those places were filled with heathens," Miss Adams stated. "Haven't we always heard that, Miss Crane?"

Miss Crane simply nodded.

"You have had a horrendous day," I sympathized. "Might I suggest you soak in the tub after supper? It will help you sleep, I am sure."

"Awk, I couldn't do that. It's not Saturday," Beulah announced. "I always take a bath on Saturday."

"It's all right. You can take one during the week, too," Calah said.

"It ain't right and natural to take more than one bath a week," Beulah stated with great conviction.

The conversation ended when Mrs. Peele and her elder daughter brought the supper.

Agatha and I sat in the back garden after supper, enjoying the cooler weather that came with the onset of autumn.

"We need to speak with Beulah," Agatha announced.

"What do we want to talk with her about?" I asked as I leaned over to sniff a pink rose.

"I want to know which ward she cleans."

"What difference does that make?"

"Were you not paying attention when she was talking about the woman who fell ill? Beulah specifically called her a lady."

I turned from the roses and stared at my friend.

"I think she works on the ward where miscreant wives are kept."

I considered Agatha's hypothesis. "That is an interesting conclusion."

The sun had dipped below the horizon, and the first stars began showing. Agatha and I went inside.

Chapter 12

30 September 1867

Agatha and I watched the gathering storm clouds as we hurried home after school.

"I'm looking forward to a lovely cup of tea before marking the homework I gave yesterday," Agatha said.

"I gave the first years a test today," I countered. "I didn't get a chance to glance through them during dinner. I'm hoping they all did well."

"I'm sure they did. You're a good teacher."

We turned up the path to the front door of the rooming house just as the first drops started to fall.

Out of habit, I glanced at the table in the foyer, saw a letter with my name on it, and picked it up.

"Put your things in your room, then come to mine. I have a letter from Ada Baumann," I instructed.

Agatha nodded and did as I asked.

I dropped my satchel on the floor next to the table, opened the envelope, and waited to read the letter until Agatha was perched on the foot of the bed.

Priscilla and Agatha,

I asked Dinah to post this letter to you. I overheard Karl and Oliver speaking Saturday after supper. Oliver said he is going to Harrisburg next month on business and has made an appointment to talk with

Elizabeth's doctors.

I pray you can use this information to locate my daughter.

Ada Baumann

"We can't ask for time off to go to Harrisburg," Agatha lamented. "How are we going to look for her so far away?"

"I will write to Gertrude Schmidt. Perhaps she can go to Harrisburg to search for Elizabeth."

"I'm certain Karl Baumann knows where Elizabeth is being held," Agatha said, pacing beside the bed. "How can he live with himself knowing his daughter is being held in one of those ghastly places?"

"He believes Elizabeth is headstrong and needs to be controlled. He told me as much last April."

Agatha closed her eyes and concentrated on resolving the problem. "I'll write to Mrs. Baumann. I owe Dinah a letter, too. Perhaps they've learned something more."

"Well, now that is settled, I am going to get a cup of tea." I placed the letter on my writing desk and pulled the test papers from my satchel before going downstairs.

Agatha followed.

Chapter 13

27 November 1867

I was hopeful when I saw Gertrude's letter on the table. Agatha and I rushed to my room to read it.

Priscilla,

I apologize for the delay in responding to your letter. I had no reason to travel to Harrisburg until last week when I met with several clients.

While there, I visited Pennsylvania Hospital for the Insane. The receptionist denied Elizabeth was in their care. However, a nurse who happened to overhear my inquiry followed me outside. She told me Elizabeth had been a patient on the "Wives Ward" but was taken away by a pair of rough-looking men at the end of August.

The nurse overheard one of the men informing the matron they were paid handsomely to take Elizabeth to Philadelphia.

I pray you will discover where Oliver has her locked up and that she is faring well.

Always,
Gertrude Schmidt

I shivered as I stared at the neatly written words on the page. "Thank you, Gertrude," I whispered.

"There's an asylum on the west side of the Schuylkill River, at 44th and Market Streets." Agatha looked at the small watch attached to her dress. "It's too late to go out today, and the streetcars won't run tomorrow."

I looked at her questioningly, then recalled that President Lincoln had issued a proclamation declaring the last Thursday in November as Thanksgiving Day in 1863. "We will go on Friday after school."

"I can't. I have an appointment with the parents of one of my students. If we go Saturday morning, we won't have to worry about returning here in time for supper."

I began removing papers from my satchel. "That is better. We can leave shortly after breakfast."

"Did you give another test?"

"No. This is third-years' homework. They were to write an original short story in French. I'm looking forward to reading them."

Agatha rose from the edge of the bed and smoothed out the counterpane. "I have homework to review as well. I hope I can get it done before supper. I have a new book I want to start reading tonight."

"What book is that?" I asked

"*The Mysterious Key.*"

"I don't know that book. Who's the author?"

"L. M. Alcott."

"Hmm. Let me know how you like it. I may borrow it."

She waved as she moved into the hallway.

Chapter 14

30 November 1867
Pennsylvania Hospital for the Insane

We arrived at the hospital at about ten o'clock in the morning. We passed through the tall arched gates and remained on a walking path with farmland on our right and the large imposing building on our left.

Fieldhands were harvesting the last of the crops while others cleared and plowed fields to be replanted in the spring.

At the far end of the building was an expanse of grass, browning after several nights of near-freezing temperatures. Hospital attendants outside accompanied several patients.

We reached the front door and approached a severe-looking man at a table near a staircase.

"How may I assist you ladies this morning?"

"Has Mrs. Elizabeth Finch been admitted as a patient?" I asked, glancing nervously at Agatha.

The man looked through a thin book, running his index finger down a list of neatly written names.

"I'm sorry, there is no patient by that name."

"How about Elizabeth Owens?"

He looked again with the same meticulous care. He shook his head.

"She may be registered as Elizabeth Baumann," I suggested.

For the third time, he shook his head. "I'm sorry."

"Thank you," Agatha said as we turned away and walked towards the front door. "That was a waste of time and streetcar fare,"

"It was not an absolute waste. We know where she is not."

We stepped on the path leading to the street. It took a few steps before I realized Agatha was not at my side.

She stood on the path, the color drained from her face, and both hands covered her mouth.

I retraced my steps and touched her arm. "What is it?"

"What if the lady was Elizabeth?" she said as she dropped her hands.

"What lady?" I asked, then remembered the story Beulah had told at supper some months ago. "Oh." I grasped Agatha's arm and guided her to the streetcar stand. "We will talk with Beulah tonight.

Beulah, Agatha, and I were the first to enter the dining room for supper and take our places at the table.

Noticing she had taken the time to change her clothes and redress her hair, I greeted her. "Good evening, Beulah. You look lovely."

"Thank you," she returned with a slight blush. "After Miss Adams chastised me about my appearance, I realized I'd been slipping into poor habits. My mother would have my hide for coming to the table looking like I'd been slopping the pigs."

"There certainly won't be any nasty remarks tonight." Agatha smiled. "We'd like to speak with you after supper."

"That would be lovely," Beulah replied, a smile meeting her eyes. "Shall we meet in the drawing room?"

"Let us meet in my room," I suggested.

She smiled broadly and did a little wiggle. "I'll be there." She quickly composed herself as Miss Adams and Miss Crane took their places.

Miss Adams glanced at Beulah and made a soft noise but said nothing.

"You look very nice tonight, Miss Snodgrass," Miss Crane said timidly.

Miss Adams glared at her friend but continued her silence.

Beulah beamed at the compliment. "Thank you, Miss Crane."

"Where is..." I started to ask about Calah but remembered she dined with her family on Friday and Saturday nights.

Supper was served and eaten without conversation.

I yielded the lone chair in my room to Beulah. Agatha and I sat on the foot of the bed, facing her.

"A few months ago, you told us of a lady at the hospital who was taken ill and died," I recalled

Beulah closed her eyes and clenched her hands together. "It was the night Miss Adams remarked about my appearance."

"Do you recall the lady's name?" Agatha asked.

"I'll never forget it. The lady was Mrs. Jane Worther."

Agatha and I released a breath.

"Do you remember Elizabeth Owens?" I asked.

"Of course." Beulah smiled. "Didn't you say she was married last spring?"

"We have been told her new husband had her committed to an asylum. We thought she was in Harrisburg, but a mutual friend informed us she was moved to a hospital in Philadelphia.

"Oh," Beulah uttered. Her head snapped up. "Of course." She jumped up, dislodging three pins from her hair, which flew across the room. "Jeanne."

"Who?" Agatha and I asked.

"Jeanne." Beulah calmed herself and resumed her seat. "Mrs. Jeanne Ziegler came in September. I thought she looked familiar but didn't recall knowing anyone by that name."

We stared at her.

A thought came to mind. I snapped my fingers and rose

from the bed to thumb through a stack of envelopes on the table. "Ah, there it is," I murmured as I removed the wedding invitation from the envelope. "There! Of course."

"What is it?" Agatha asked.

"'Elizabeth Jeanne Owens,'" I read. "Elizabeth's middle name is Jeanne. It must be her." I turned to face Beulah. "Do you work tomorrow?"

"No. I don't work on Sundays," she informed us.

"Would you be willing to ask Jeanne whether she is Elizabeth Jeanne Finch?" Finch is her new husband's name," I explained.

"I'm certain she is," Beulah said. "I'll speak with her on Monday. She's such a lovely lady, always kind to the staff."

"Is there anything we may do for you?" I asked.

"Not a thing." She sat quietly for a moment. "Elizabeth. Yes, I'm certain Jeanne is your friend."

We were all on our feet and edging towards the door.

"I wonder whether there's any more pumpkin pie," Agatha pondered, leading us downstairs.

Chapter 15

2 December 1867
Mrs. Peele's Boardinghouse

"Thank heaven, this day is nearly over," Agatha said as we hurried home in the drizzly rain that threatened to turn to snow.

"Beulah will not be home until after six o'clock," I pointed out. "I could barely concentrate enough to teach. How will I keep busy for the next three or four hours?"

"I've had the same problem. But we must endure." Agatha opened the door and closed it after we entered the house.

"Oh, warm and dry," I whispered and went to my room.

I exchanged concerned glances with Agatha when Beulah wasn't at supper and prayed for her safety.

We were finishing supper when the front door opened, and someone stumbled into the foyer.

I glimpsed Beulah on the stairs and excused myself from the table to follow her. "Beulah, are you ill?"

She did not respond but continued to her room.

I followed. "Whatever is the matter?" I asked, closing the door behind me. "Did another patient die?"

"No, no. Nothing like that," Beulah said, removing her soaking-wet cape and hanging it on a hook. "I got on the streetcar at the usual time, but the weather was terrible, and a delivery van became mired in the mud, blocking the road. As the streetcar driver was working to move around the van, a farm wagon appeared and spooked the horses. They shied away and broke their harness, leaving the streetcar in the middle of the road.

"There was nothing for it but to walk to the nearest streetcar stand and hope there would be a connection to bring us across the river. We had to walk nearly a quarter mile on the muddy roads."

"Oh, Beulah. That is terrible. Let us get you out of those wet clothes and into bed. I will go down and bring your supper to you."

She stared at me and began to cry. "Why are you being so nice to me?"

"Because you need help. I would do the same for Miss Adams if she would allow it." I went to the chest of drawers and found a nightdress, then helped her out of the wet and muddy dress and underpinnings.

When she was settled in bed, I discovered that Mrs. Peele had prepared a tray.

I knocked softly on Beulah's door and opened it. The woman was sound asleep. I returned the tray to the kitchen and went to my room.

Chapter 16

6 December 1867

Beulah didn't talk with Agatha and me until after supper on Friday. "I wasn't able to talk with Jeanne until this afternoon. The admittance documents show her name as Mrs. Jeanne Ziegler."

"I think Ziegler is her mother's maiden name," Agatha related.

"She was moved to a private room yesterday. I went there to clean the floor. She remembers me and confirmed she is your friend, Elizabeth."

Agatha and I smiled broadly and hugged the bearer of the news.

"We shall go visit her Saturday," I declared. "Thank you, Beulah. Elizabeth's family will be relieved to know she is well."

We agreed to keep the news to ourselves until after we'd seen Elizabeth.

"We must devise a plan to get her out of there," Agatha observed.

Being pragmatic, I said, "Let us not get ahead of ourselves. We must first meet with Elizabeth and assure ourselves she is well."

Chapter 17

7 December 1867
Pennsylvania Hospital for the Insane

Agatha and I presented ourselves at the asylum, confident we now had the correct name and would soon be visiting with our friend.

"We'd like to see Mrs. Jeanne Ziegler, please," Agatha proclaimed to the same severe-looking man we'd previously encountered.

He performed his investigation of the book before him and looked up with a smug grin. "Mrs. Ziegler is not permitted visitors under any circumstance. You must leave."

We stared at him in disbelief. "Why is she not allowed to have visitors?" Agatha asked.

"She would certainly be delighted to see us," I countered.

"It says here she's not allowed to see anyone except her husband," he replied.

"Thank you," Agatha said and steered me towards the door. Once outside, she turned to me. "There was nothing to be gained by arguing with that man. We'll talk with Beulah and determine how to overcome this obstacle."

I sagged slightly. "Yes, I suppose we must. At least we can write to Mrs. Baumann and Dinah. They will be relieved to learn we know she is in Philadelphia."

We trudged back to the streetcar stand and waited to return to the other side of the river.

I looked back for a last glance at the asylum and whispered,

"We will get you out of there, Elizabeth. I promise,"

Chapter 18

8 December 1867
Mrs. Peele's Boardinghouse

Beulah sat on my bed with Agatha beside her. I paced the room, relating the tale of our thwarted attempt to visit Elizabeth.

"That would be Mr. Evans. He is a most unpleasant man," Beulah informed us.

"He seemed to take a perverse pleasure in turning us away," Agatha said.

"I don't think he likes women," Beulah mused.

"What if we were to write to Elizabeth?" Agatha asked.

"I've never seen her receive any letters, but that could be because her husband was the only person who knew where she was." Beulah paused briefly. "She was taking air with an attendant but hasn't since the weather turned. But, now that she has a private room, I can pass messages to her."

I stared at the cleaner. "That could be dangerous for you, would it not?"

"I am very careful."

Agatha and I exchanged a glance.

"You have done this before?" I asked

Beulah didn't respond but raised her eyebrows and gave us a sheepish grin.

"We wouldn't want any harm to come to either you or Elizabeth," Agatha stated.

"I've carried messages to other patients," Beulah admitted. "What would you have me say to Jeanne?"

"Tell her that now we know where she is, we will be working

out how to free her from that dreadful place," I said.

"I change her bed linen on Tuesdays. That will be the best day to have a private word with her." Beulah stood and smoothed the front of her dress. "We'll meet back here Tuesday after supper."

"Thank you, Beulah. We're indebted to you." Agatha hugged the plump woman and kissed her cheek.

"I've not done anything just yet," Beulah countered. "Jeanne has always been kind to me. I'll help you however I can." She stepped towards the door. "Good night."

Agatha and I heard footfalls in the hall and the closing of a door.

"And so, we wait," I intoned and sat in the chair while Agatha resumed her place at the foot of the bed.

Chapter 19

10 December 1867

I was passing through the foyer to the drawing room when Beulah returned from the hospital.

She smiled and nodded as she moved towards the staircase.

I chose a chair near the door, which was left open.

Miss Adams was seated in the drawing room near the fireplace. "I must wonder what you and Miss Bentley have in common with Miss Snodgrass. It's been noticed the three of you are thick as thieves these past weeks,"

"Miss Snodgrass and I are renewing our acquaintance," I replied curtly. "We must talk in the evenings since she works longer hours. I would suppose we will go for walks on Sundays when weather permits."

"Then you knew Miss Snodgrass before you came to live here?"

I took my sewing from the basket I had been carrying and began stitching a seam on a pair of drawers. "I met her when I lived here before, but we did not have the opportunity to become better acquainted."

"I'm told you and your friend were quite unsociable."

"Miss Adams, you have made it quite clear you disapprove of me. I am not obligated to explain myself or Mrs. Owens to you or anyone else. I will tell you the events of the past twenty months were harrowing. I returned to Philadelphia to start a new life." I placed my sewing back in the basket and rose from the chair. "I do not believe I have given you any reason to dislike me. I recommend you recall Matthew, chapter 7: [1]*Judge not, lest ye be judged.* [2]*For what judgment ye judge, ye shall be judged, and what measure ye mete, it shall be measured to you again.*" I turned my back on the unpleasant woman, intent on returning to my room.

"You are correct, Miss Llewellyn. I have judged you without having met you or knowing anything about you save what I've garnered from the people who know you."

"Perhaps you ought not to believe everything you hear." I returned to my room, slammed the door, dropped the sewing basket on the table, threw myself on the bed, and cried into my pillow.

"What on earth is the matter?" Beula asked, standing beside the bed.

I had not heard her come in, and I took a moment to compose myself before turning over to look at my new friend. "I allowed Miss Adams to get the better of me." I withdrew the handkerchief from my sleeve and mopped my face. I sat up and looked at the portly lady.

Beulah leaned over and hugged me. "That woman is bitter and mean. I don't know why, and I don't want to know. Ignore her."

"I know. It does not make it any easier when her vitriol is directed at me."

Beulah sat on the edge of the bed and grasped my hands. "I've always thought of you as brave and strong."

A derisive laugh escaped me as Agatha came to the open door. "What's happened?" She was still wearing her hat and gloves. "Miss Adams is downstairs demanding Mrs. Peele turn you out."

Beulah and I groaned.

I shook my head and dabbed my eyes one last time.

"Perhaps Mrs. Peele will turn out Miss Adams," Beulah said softly.

The three of us exchanged glances, then broke into giggles.

"Agatha put away your things and come back," I instructed.

While she was gone, Beulah and I arranged ourselves on the bed to make room for Agatha.

Miss Adams, Miss Crane, and Calah Sheftall were already seated when the three of us took our places at the supper table.

"Good evening," Calah greeted.

"Good evening. I trust you have had a good day," I said.

"It has been a very good day. One of my students who has been struggling in Hebrew class did very well today."

"It's always rewarding when concepts suddenly make sense to a struggling student," Agatha said.

"Have you been working with her?" I asked.

"No. I think her father has been, though. She pronounced a few words differently than I do, and I've heard him pronounce them as she did."

"It's nice when parents take an interest in their daughters' educations," Beulah observed. "My mother helped me to learn to read and write and insisted I learn to speak properly. Papa didn't see the point of educating a girl beyond being able to cook and clean."

"Everyone knows..." Miss Adams started.

Miss Crane glared at her and touched her arm.

Miss Adams resumed eating without finishing her sentence.

Beulah, Calah, Agatha, and I exchanged confused looks and continued eating.

After supper, we assembled in Beulah's room.

"Me thinks Miss Adams was told to behave," Agatha said,

failing at her attempt to stifle her giggles.

"That is the impression I have." Beulah sat in the chair while Agatha and I perched on the foot of the bed.

"Are you going to keep us in suspense?" I asked.

"Jeanne is relieved that you two know where she is and wants to see you. But she sees no end to her confinement as long as the court deems her insane."

"Then, it's time to talk with one of Calah's uncles," I announced. "I'll ask her to help us make an appointment. We'll bring all the letters and tell him what we know. There must be some way for Elizabeth to help herself."

"Does she go outside?" Agatha asked.

"Not since the first snowfall," Beulah replied.

"We don't dare go back to ask to visit with her," I mused. "We shall have to bide our time until Elizabeth walks the grounds again."

"In the meantime, I'll continue to relay messages," Beulah announced.

A knock on the door interrupted the conversation.

"Come in," Beulah called out.

Calah stood in the open doorway, taking in the scene. "I'm sorry. I didn't intend to interrupt."

"Come in and sit with us," Beulah invited.

"Thank you." Calah sat nearest to the door, next to Agatha.

"It's nice of you to join us," Agatha said.

"I wanted to find out what's happened. Miss Crane is in the drawing room, and Miss Adams is in her room making all manner of noises. It sounds as though she's throwing things and speaking rather unintelligibly.

Calah had our attention.

"Miss Adams and Priscilla had words this afternoon, after which we're given to understand Miss Adams made an appeal to turn out Priscilla," Beulah explained.

"Perhaps Miss Adams was turned out," Agatha surmised.

"Do you suppose we ought to go downstairs to 'console' Miss Crane?" I asked.

A few moments passed before Agatha caught my meaning and grinned. "Yes, I'm certain Miss Crane is bereft of her friend leaving the house."

The four of us filed out of the room and downstairs. We found Miss Crane alone in the drawing room. She stared into the fire with an open book on her lap. Most notably, her eyes were dry, and she exuded an air of contentment. She turned her head at the scroop of our skirts. "Come in, ladies, and sit with me."

I was taken with her delicate British accent.

"Barbara is in a right state. It's best to leave her to settle down. She fancies herself always in control. It infuriates her when someone bests her or refuses to abide by her wishes."

"Has Mrs. Peele turned her out?" Beulah timidly asked.

A deprecating laugh escaped the older woman. "If only she had. Alas, no. Mrs. Peele told her if she was unhappy here, she was free to leave."

My admiration for Mrs. Peele grew exponentially.

"Would anyone else like a cup of tea?" Calah asked.

"I'd rather something stronger," Miss Crane replied. "But tea would be lovely."

"There may be pie or cake, too," Beulah suggested. "I'll go with you, Calah."

They moved towards the kitchen while Agatha and I sat in chairs near Miss Crane.

"It sounds as though Miss Adams is having a tantrum," Agatha reported.

"I'm afraid she is prone to throwing things when she doesn't get her way." Miss Crane explained.

"That's awful," I uttered.

"I suppose Mrs. Peele or her daughters will be charged with cleaning her room tomorrow."

"Oh, no. After the second time she did it, Mrs. Peele told Barbara to clear away the mess herself. Her rent was raised, and Barbara had to pay for the damages to the walls and furniture."

"What was that?" Calah asked, carrying a tray laden with the tea things.

Beulah followed with a tray bearing gingerbread fresh from the oven, with plates, napkins, and forks.

"Oh, what a treat," Miss Crane exclaimed when handed a plate.

We savored the warm gingerbread and hot tea without any conversation. The sounds from upstairs ceased, and we looked at one another, wondering whether Miss Adams had demolished all her possessions or was simply exhausted.

Mrs. Peele came in bearing another pot of tea.

"Thank you," Miss Crane said. "You are very kind, Mrs. Peele."

"It's lovely to see my boarders enjoying the company of one another," the landlady replied.

Beulah placed her empty plate, cup, and saucer on a tray. "I'm going up," she informed us. She was halfway across the room when she stopped and turned around. "Oh, I forgot to tell you. I must work Sunday but will be off on Wednesday."

"Just next week?" I asked.

"No, every Wednesday, for a while. Good night, ladies. It's been a most informative evening." She turned and made her way upstairs.

"I suppose we should retire as well," I suggested. "The students will expect us to be coherent in classes tomorrow." I turned to Miss Crane. "It's been lovely chatting with you. I hope we may have more conversations."

"Good night, Miss Llewellyn. This has been a most enjoyable evening."

Agatha and Calah also bade good night and followed me upstairs.

Part 2
Unexpected Events

Chapter 20

9 January 1868

Christmas and New Year had come and gone with little fanfare at Mrs. Peele's boardinghouse.

Agatha, Calah, and I returned to our daily and weekly routines.

Beulah carried messages from and to Elizabeth. We were all anxious for spring when we could visit her again.

When Agatha and I returned from school, a letter from Melissa Brandt, one of my closest friends in Norwich, Connecticut, lay on the foyer table. I rushed to my room and divested myself of my satchel and outer clothes before settling on the bed to read what I anticipated to be a newsy letter.

I was disappointed to find a single sheet of paper with just a few lines written on it.

Priscilla,

It is with great sorrow that I write to inform you Marian Morrison passed in her sleep on the third of January. We're all going to miss your godmother. I have lovely memories of house parties in her home when we were younger.

I'll write soon with happier news.

Your friend,
Melissa

Tears streamed down my face and onto Melissa's letter. Memories played in my head—dinner parties with my friends and their mothers, long conversations with Aunt Marian, and my eighteenth birthday party, where I was introduced to society. Aunt Marian chastised me for shirking my responsibilities as mistress of Riverbend, then taught me what I needed to know. She also championed Ethan Brandt as my suitor.

No one came to my door as I wept quietly for the woman who helped raise me. She was always my champion and sometimes bullied my father to allow me to participate in social activities appropriate for a young lady of our social class.

I prayed she was safely in Heaven with her husband and my mother. *Is Papa there, too?*

A clock chimed the three-quarter hour.

I splashed water on my face, patted my hair into place, smoothed my dress, and placed a clean, dry handkerchief in my pocket before going downstairs to supper.

Chapter 21

20 January 1868

When we arrived home from school, Agatha and I were laughing over an anecdote she was telling about a student in one of her classes.

"Oh, look, Priscilla, you have a letter." Agatha handed the envelope to me.

The return address read "Law Office of Nathaniel Osborne" in Norwich. Trepidation washed over me. *Is Papa alive?* I hurried to my room to read the letter.

Miss Llewellyn:

My deepest condolences for the loss of your godmother, Marian Morrison. I have included a copy of her Last Will and Testament. She left the majority of her estate to you, with small bequests to the First Congregational Church, friends, and servants. Please make arrangements to come to my office in Norwich to review the details of your inheritance.

Best Regards,
Nathaniel Osborne
Attorney at Law

The letter flittered to the floor as the envelope containing the copy of the will landed with a soft thud. *Aunt Marian left everything to me?*

I sat heavily on the edge of the bed, repeating the contents of the letter in my mind. *I wonder how extensive her estate is.*

"Priscilla, are you all right?" Agatha asked through the door.

"What? Oh, yes, yes," I stumbled over my words. "Come in."

She took in my appearance. "Have you had bad news?"

"On the contrary. Most people will say it is very good news." I got off the bed and stooped to pick up the letter and envelope.

I handed the letter to her.

Her eyes widened as she read it. Agatha looked at me. "When are you leaving?"

"I am not. I will write to Mr. Osborne to explain that I cannot travel to Connecticut until June. I will go to Norwich when the spring term ends. The visit should not be overlong. We must do what we can to help Elizabeth leave that awful place."

She handed back the letter.

I folded it and returned it to the envelope. "Truth be told, I never thought I would return to Norwich." I stared at the letter in my hand. "Papa sold our home and sailed to Africa. Then, he sent me to Texas."

"What about your childhood friends? You've spoken of them several times."

"They have their own families and lives." I set the envelope on the table and turned to sit on the edge of the bed. Agatha sat beside me. "I wrote to Melissa Brand and Rachel Downs three times after I left Norwich. They could not reply because I did not provide a return address."

"It will be wonderful to see them all again. I will return to Philadelphia as soon as I have finished my business with Mr. Osborne."

Agatha smiled. "You now own what I am certain is a beautiful house."

"A home that holds memories better left alone," I said harshly. The image of Ethan Brandt standing at the foot of the stairs and sweeping me off my feet before kissing me and announcing Papa had given us his blessing to wed flashed in my mind. "It's much too large for a spinster."

"Wasn't your godmother a widow?"

"Yes, but she lived in that house long before her husband died. I was told it was her childhood home."

"My point is, she lived alone in that house with her memories."

"That is true." I sighed. "I am glad I will have time to prepare myself before I return to Norwich."

Agatha rose. "I'll leave you to write your letter. I'm off to devise the test I'm giving on Friday. " She turned in the doorway. "Don't make any hasty decisions."

I sat at the table, withdrew Mr. Osborne's letter from the envelope, and reread it. *There are so many painful memories for me in Norwich. I do not want to live in the past.*

Taking a sheet of my stationary, I opened the ink pot, took up my pen, and began to write.

Chapter 22

10 February 1868

Beulah came home from work and ran upstairs.

"Why are you in such a hurry?" I asked, meeting her at the top of the stairs.

"I want to talk with you and Agatha before supper, and I need to change my dress."

"It's only six o'clock. You have sufficient time to change and talk with us. We'll meet in my room when you are done dressing." I continued downstairs on my errand.

Back upstairs, I stopped at Agatha's room. "Beulah wants to talk. We'll be in my room."

Agatha dropped her pencil on the table and looked at me. "Your timing is impeccable. I just finished marking papers." She rose and stretched her back, then followed me into my room.

Beulah was not far behind."I wanted you to know Elizabeth is not well. She's taken to her bed. One of the doctors came to examine her and said she'd recover, but she must remain in bed for a few days.

"Is she feverish?" Agatha asked.

"I don't know. I wasn't in her room today. I only know what Mrs. Davidson told me. Tomorrow is my day to clean her floor. If I'm allowed in, I'll speak with her."

"Thank you for telling us. Please convey our best wishes," Agatha said.

"Has her husband been told?" I asked.

"I don't know. I'll ask Mrs. Davidson. I think I saw him at

the hospital on Saturday."

Agatha and I exchanged glances. "And she's ill today." I mused.

"She fell ill Saturday night after I had left for the day," Beulah stated.

"The day he'd been to see her," Agatha uttered. "Did they have words?"

"I don't think so. He brought her a bag of sweets. She shared them with some of the other ladies."

Agatha and I perked up.

"Sweets?" I repeated.

"What kind of sweets?" Agatha asked.

"I didn't see them. Mrs. Davidson said..."

"We need to speak with Irene Davidson," Agatha declared.

"When? Where?" I asked.

"Wednesday. At the park near Forty-eighth Street," Agatha said. "We can be there by four o'clock if we take a cab from the school."

Chapter 23

12 February 1868

The cab dropped us off at the park with fifteen minutes to spare and followed Mrs. Davidson into the park.

"Good afternoon," she greeted as she turned her head to look behind her.

"Thank you for meeting with us," I replied. "It will be dark soon so we won't keep you long. We have questions about Elizabeth."

"Mrs. Ziegler is recovered from whatever ailed her," the attendant reported.

"Beulah told us Oliver visited her last Saturday and brought some sort of sweets. Do you suspect they were tainted?" I asked.

Mrs. Davidson smiled. "Not much gets past you, Miss Llewellyn. Yes, I believe the sweets were tainted, as you say. One of the other ladies on the ward ate one and also fell ill with the same symptoms. Mr. Ziegler will be asked to refrain from bringing food to her in the future."

"That is a relief," Agatha breathed.

Mrs. Davidson looked at her watch and the sky. "It is getting late, and it appears we may be in for a storm. I will pass on any information through Beulah."

The three of us hurried back to the street and said our farewells. Agatha and I were able to catch a streetcar back to the other side of the river and the boardinghouse.

Chapter 24

"Oh, look, a letter for you," Calah said as I passed through the foyer to the kitchen.

"Thank you, Calah," I said, taking the envelope from her and glancing at the return address. *Mr. Nathaniel Osborne. Now, what do you want of me?* I continued on my errand. "Is the kettle hot?" I asked Faith, Mrs. Peele's younger daughter.

"Yes. Would you like a pot to take to your room?" She stopped snapping beans and hopped off the stool where she'd been sitting.

I pointed to a teapot on the draining board. "There is a pot already brewed. I'll pour out a cup."

"That one's been sitting since dinner and has likely gone cold. It's no problem to brew a fresh pot." She quickly brewed tea in a clean pot and set up a tray for me to take to my room.

"Thank you so much," I said, placing the envelope on the tray before picking it up.

"You're welcome." The girl resumed snapping beans.

Upstairs, I placed the tray on the table, picked up the envelope, and slipped my letter opener under the sealing wax.

Dear Miss Llewellyn:

In light of your inability to travel to Norwich, I am sending an associate to you. Mr. Bartholomew Martin will arrive in Philadelphia on the evening of Friday, 13 March. He will call on you on the fourteenth at nine o'clock in the morning to apprise you of your inheritance and assist in completing transfers of ownership to you.

Best regards,
Nathaniel Osborne
Attorney-at-Law

"Bartholomew Martin," I whispered as I sat heavily on the bed. I remembered him vividly. His family lived on the farm northwest of Riverbend, my childhood home. It would *be good to see him again.*

I set aside Mr. Osborne's letter, poured a cup of tea, and sat at the table to read the stories my fourth-year students had written.

Chapter 25

14 March 1868

Bartholomew Martin, Esquire, arrived at the rooming house at nine o'clock in the morning. I received him in the drawing room.

"Good morning, Bartholomew," I said, holding out my hand to him.

"Good morning, Priscilla. I wasn't certain you'd remember me." He took my hand and held it briefly.

"How could I forget the Martin boys? You and Mark taught me to climb the trees by the river."

He shook his head. "And got our hides tanned for the effort. How were we to know girls weren't meant to climb trees? We didn't have any sisters."

"I wasn't allowed outside for a week afterward." I rolled my eyes. "I was seven and endured lectures on the comportment of young Ladies' for the next eleven years."

We shared a laugh, then settled to the task at hand.

"Mrs. Morrison's passing saddens me. She was always so nice to my brothers and me. I liked her," Bartholomew said.

"She was a remarkable woman and knew how to convince Papa to do her bidding," I recalled.

"Well, she's left you her house in Norwich."

"Oh, the library," I exclaimed. "All those lovely books..."

"Are yours," he finished my sentence. "You can sequester yourself in the library and never leave. You also have her carriage and horses."

I looked up. "Is there a driver?"

"Yes. Mrs. Morrison's servants have stayed and care for the house, gardens, carriages, and livestock. In addition to the horses, there's a cow and a flock of chickens."

"What about Peanut?" I asked.

"The cat's name is 'Peanut?'"

I smiled. "She was so tiny and the color of a peanut when she was born."

He laughed. "She certainly grew out of that name. She must weigh fifteen pounds."

"Yes, she did grow larger than we expected. But she knew her name by then, and we couldn't change it."

"Well, at least her color is the same." He scanned the page in his hand. "Peanut is yours as well." He looked at me. "How old is she?"

I closed my eyes, trying to remember when she was born. "Let me see. It was before the war…. It must have been '57 or '58. That would make her about ten years old."

He shook his head. "I don't think we ever had a cat live that long."

"Yours were barn cats. So were ours. Papa would not allow them inside the house," I reminisced.

Bartholomew turned the page. "The servants have been told you are the new owner of the house."

"Have they been paid? I would hate to think of them working without getting their wages."

"As executor, Mr. Osborne has kept up with Mrs. Morrison's expenses, including payroll.

"I have several documents for you to sign." Bartholomew pulled out a sheaf of papers and set them on the table. He patiently explained each one and asked me to sign it when he was confident I understood.

It was nearly dinnertime when our business was concluded.

"Would you like to join us for dinner?" I asked. "I'm certain Mrs. Peele would not mind."

"Thank you. I was rather hoping you would be agreeable to taking your dinner with me at a restaurant.

I looked up, surprised at the invitation. "I would like that very much. I had not realized how much I miss my friends in Norwich until this morning." I rose from the chair and moved towards the door. "I will inform Mrs. Peele that I will not be dining in and go up to gather my things."

Mrs. Peele was quite understanding, and five minutes later, Bartholomew Martin and I were on the curbstone, hailing a cab.

Once settled at a table at Fennimore's Restaurant, we perused the menu and placed our orders.

"I have never eaten here before," I said, looking around at the décor.

"Our law clerk recommended it to me. He lived in Philadelphia most of his life."

"How did he come to live in Norwich?"

"He attended Yale College and applied for a clerkship. Mr. Osborne was impressed."

The waiter delivered our meals, and we each took a bite before continuing our conversation.

"How did you come to be in Philadelphia? Mr. Osborne thought you were in Corpus Christi, Texas," Bartholomew asked.

"That is a very long story. Suffice it to say Mr. Pennyman and I were not well suited to one another. He met with an untimely demise the day before I left Corpus Christi." I hesitated, then asked, "How did Mr. Osborne discover my whereabouts?"

Bartholomew considered this information as he ate. "You wrote to Melissa Brandt when you took up residency in Philadelphia. She told her parents. I presume Mr. Brandt told Mr. Osborne. My employer would be interested in your story."

"I suppose I must relate it at least one more time after I return to Norwich."

"When do you propose to go to Norwich?"

"I cannot travel until the end of the term in June."

"I shall look forward to you coming home," he said.

"Not to disappoint, but I do not plan to remain in Norwich. I have made Philadelphia my home. I must return before the start of the autumn school term, and I have a friend who is in a precarious situation."

Discouragement was writ on his face. "Of course. I understand."

We finished the meal and ordered dessert.

"How is your family?" I asked. "Are your mother and father enjoying living at Riverbend?"

"I'm uncertain. Mother was uncomfortable at first, but she loved having all those bedrooms for the orphans she collected during the war. Father took it in stride. My younger brothers and I remained at Martin Farm. I moved to town shortly after Mr. Osborne hired me in 1866."

"Are any of the orphans still living with your parents?"

"Most of them have left. After the war, some went to live with other family members. Many of the boys struck out on their own when they came of age. Four girls at Riverbend are learning domestic skills. The other girls have secured employment in other cities."

"Goodness." I decided to turn the conversation. "Are you acquainted with Philip Brandt?"

"Yes. I've known Philip for years. We were in school together in Norwich and took a few classes together at Yale. Did you know he's now working at his father's bank?"

"I did not, but I am also not surprised. I was very close to the Brandt family," I admitted quietly.

He became somber. "Weren't you betrothed to his cousin, Ethan?"

I nodded, uncertain of my voice.

"My belated condolences. I knew Ethan quite well. He was considering reading for the law. It was a great shock when I learned he was killed in battle in 1865."

"I was devastated. I thought I would never love again."

"That statement implies you did."

"Yes, briefly. There was never any future with the gentlemen, though. We were too different."

"I'm sorry to hear that."

We finished our dessert, and Bartholomew paid the bill.

Outside, the day was sunny and warmer than usual for March.

"Would you care for a stroll?" he asked.

"That would be lovely," I replied. "There is a charming park not far from here."

He held out his arm for me. "Lead the way, m'lady."

Bartholomew returned me to the boardinghouse around four o'clock.

"It's been a lovely afternoon. Thank you," I said, looking into his face.

"I've enjoyed our time together. I'm not leaving for New York until Monday morning. May I see you tomorrow?"

I attempted to conceal my delight at the request. "Certainly. My friend and I will be attending church services in the morning."

"Where do you worship?"

"Christ Church on American Street."

"I may see you at church. Good afternoon, Priscilla." He smiled and bowed slightly before stepping back while I entered the house.

I shut the door, leaned against it, and closed my eyes. *What am I doing?*

Shortly after I entered my room, Agatha and Beulah came in, peppering me with questions.

"So, tell us everything," Agatha demanded

"Bartholomew Martin works for Aunt Marian's attorney," I explained.

"We know that," Agatha said impatiently.

"Bartholomew has three brothers. The older one is married and made a homestead claim in the State of Missouri. The younger two remained at Martin Farm after their father purchased Riverbend. The two farms share a common border."

"He's handsome and seems nice," Agatha observed.

"He is," I agreed.

"Where did he take you for dinner?" Beulah leaned forward.

"Fennimore's Restaurant."

"Oh, I heard something about that restaurant not long ago," Agatha recalled.

"Where is it?" Beulah asked.

"It's on South Street near Second," I explained. "I had never been there, but the food was quite good. We ought to have dinner there some afternoon when we are all home."

"Perhaps you'll see Mr. Martin when you go home in June." Beulah's voice had a dreamy quality.

"I am certain he will be much too busy to pay attention to me," I asserted, secretly hoping he would be a frequent visitor to Aunt Marian's house. I glanced at the watch pinned to my dress. "It's nearly time for supper."

We trooped down together and sat in the drawing room until the clock chimed seven.

Chapter 26

15 March 1868

Agatha and I sat in a pew near the back of the sanctuary. We said our silent prayers and opened hymnals to the first hymn posted on the hymn board at the front near the altar.

The organist was playing a hymn with which I was unfamiliar, and I was curious to learn the title and lyrics.

Bartholomew slipped into the pew and positioned himself to my left, with a space for two other people between us.

I acknowledged him with a nod and a smile as the first measures of the processional hymn were played.

Agatha and I waited patiently as the people in the pews in front of us filed into the center aisle and out of the sanctuary.

Bartholomew moved closer to me. "Good morning, Miss Lewellyn, Miss Bentley."

"It is a lovely morning, Mr. Martin," I returned. "I trust you passed a restful night. I know how difficult it can be when one is away from home."

"I did indeed," he replied.

"It is good to see you again," Agatha offered and looked away to evaluate the progress of emptying the pews.

"What are your plans for the remainder of the day?" I asked.

"I'm uncertain. I had originally thought we would still be reviewing legal documents. Have you plans for the afternoon?"

I glanced at Agatha, whose attention was averted to

something on the other side of the church. "I had not made plans for the day. I will likely while away the afternoon reading. I recently purchased a few French novels and am looking forward to reading them."

"Would you favor me with a stroll this afternoon?"

Agatha smiled and touched my arm. "Yes," she whispered, preparing to join the line in the center aisle.

"I will look forward to strolling with you," I admitted and followed Agatha.

Bartholomew was right behind me.

After greeting The Reverand Benjamin Dorr, I introduced Bartholomew. They spoke briefly before the couple returned to the boardinghouse.

Mrs. Peele invited Bartholomew to join us for brunch. He graciously declined. Turning to me, he promised to return at two o'clock.

Bartholomew and I walked to a nearby park and watched boys playing Crack the Whip while girls sat on blankets under trees, reading or playing with dolls.

"Oh, to be young again with few cares in this world," I mused.

"After the animals were fed and we'd been to church, my brothers and I were free to do as we pleased," Bartholomew recalled.

"What did you do?"

"When the weather was fine, we went outside and played games or went fishing. When we had to stay indoors, we read or drew pictures. Sometimes we played card games. We frequently played pranks on one another."

"Didn't you ever disagree?"

"Of course. We were brothers, and brothers have different opinions. Sometimes, we fought with words instead of our fists."

We strolled in silence, watching the children and adults.

As we left the park, Bartholomew casually asked, "May I write to you?"

I gave him a sideways glance, smiled and nodded. "Yes, I would like that."

"Will you write back?" Concern was in his voice and writ on his face.

"Of course," I said lightly.

He did a little jig as we crossed the street and grinned broadly as we walked to the front door of the rooming house.

Chapter 27

10 April 1868

The days grew warmer and longer as winter turned to spring. Beulah arrived at supper with a twinkle in her eye and a smile brightening her round face.

"You're much too cheerful," Miss Adams complained. "Good Friday is a solemn day to remember our Savior perishing on the cross."

"I'm sorry," Beulah replied. "I received news about a friend." She directed a shallow nod towards Agatha and me.

Her news must have something to do with Elizabeth. I nodded back.

Miss Adams glared at me and changed the subject. "I suppose you'll be leaving us soon, Miss Llewellyn."

"And why would that be?" I asked, pointedly looking at her.

"A very attractive young man recently visited you. It stands to reason that you will leave to be with him."

I laughed. "You labor under a false impression. The gentleman is an attorney. He brought documents for me to sign. There is nothing between us."

"So you say. Miss Crane and I heard you laughing and addressing him by his Christian name. And I saw an envelope addressed to you on the foyer table. His name was in the return address. He is obviously interested in you."

"My relationship with the gentleman is none of your affair. We are acquaintances, that is all."

"So you say," she muttered and resumed eating.

Upstairs, in Agatha's room, Beulah grinned broadly. "A letter from Mr. Martin?"

"Yes. He wrote to assure me he arrived safely in Norwich and that Mr. Osborne was pleased all the documents had been signed," I related, trying hard not to show my delight at receiving the letter.

"Will you respond?" Agatha asked.

"Of course." I quirked the corners of my mouth.

"Beulah, tell us your news," Agatha urged.

"I have it on good authority that Jeanne will be walking outside tomorrow morning. You should be at the Ladies' Pleasure Ground behind the hospital after ten o'clock. There is a bench under an Oak tree. Jeanne will meet you there."

Agatha squealed.

I gasped. All thought of Bartholomew Martin was banished as I anticipated meeting with Elizabeth.

"Patients are required to have an attendant when they are outside." Beulah added. "Mrs. Davidson will be walking with her,"

"Is this Mrs. Davidson to be trusted?" I asked warily.

"Most certainly. She's very kind and quite critical of the treatment our patients receive. Though she vehemently denies it, she's helped other women gain their freedom."

"We'll be there," Agatha stated.

"Be aware that Jeanne looks very different than when you last saw her. She's lost a great deal of weight."

"Don't they feed those women?" I asked.

"The food served to the patients isn't of the best quality, poorly prepared, and the portions are quite small."

"That is terrible. Might we bring food for her?" I asked.

"It would be taken from her and eaten by the staff." Beulah shook her head. "The women on this ward are not treated as sorely as those on other wards, but some of the staff take advantage of them all the same."

"I can hardly believe we will see Elizabeth tomorrow," I murmured.

Chapter 28

11 April 1868
Pennsylvania Hospital for the Insane

There was a chill in the air as Agatha and I made our way to the street car that would take us to the asylum. We were nervous and excited.

The ride to the hospital was uneventful, with few other riders this day before Easter.

Agatha squeezed my hand after we disembarked and started towards the hospital entrance on Haverford Road. "What time is it?"

I looked at my watch. "a quarter past ten."

We hastened our steps and were soon through the gate, past the hospital building, and at the Ladies' Pleasure Ground. Seeing no oak tree, we followed the walking path around to the back of the three-story building to another Ladies' Pleasure Ground. There, we found a bench under a venerable oak tree.

We sat, catching our breath after the brisk walk. Several women patients, their nightdresses showing at the open neck of their dressing gowns, strolled with attendants.

"There's the bench." Agatha indicated to our left. She grasped my wrist and pulled me along at a brisk pace.

Shortly after settling under the oak tree, we observed several women wearing day dresses perambulating around the side of the building. A hospital attendant accompanied each. One woman broke from the group and came towards us.

I recognized the dress as a favorite of Elizabeth's and forced myself to remain seated until the woman and her attendant were nearer.

"Priscilla? Agatha?" Elizabeth queried.

We rose and took several steps towards her.

"It is grand to see you," I responded, working to keep the shock of her altered appearance out of my voice.

Her dress hung shapelessly from her shoulders, and she was not wearing a crinoline. Elizabeth had pleated the neckline and affixed it with a brooch to reduce its size.

The woman in the blue uniform dress stepped forward and held out her right hand. "I'm Mrs. Irene Davidson. You are Miss Llewellyn and Miss Bentley?"

"I'm Agatha." She took the woman's hand. "It's nice to meet you."

"Please, call me Priscilla," I said as I took her hand.

"I am aware of her true identity, but you should address her as Mrs. Jeanne Ziegler. That is the name by which she has been admitted to our care."

"Please, sit with us," I offered.

"She is outside for exercise," Mrs. Davidson advised. "Please walk with us."

Agatha and I positioned Elizabeth between us. Mrs. Davidson followed at a respectful distance.

"I'm so pleased to see you both," Elizabeth looked from Agatha to me. "I never thought Oliver would go through with his threat, but here I am."

"With your permission, we want to talk with an attorney about having you adjudged sane," Agatha informed her.

Elizabeth shook her head. "I have all but lost hope of ever being free."

"Has Oliver been successful in gaining control of your money?" I asked.

"No, and he is furious." Elizabeth looked over her shoulder at Mrs. Davidson, then turned back. "Did you get my letter from Mr. McConnaughy? I arranged for everything to be placed in trusts."

"Yes, I believe you to be quite clever," I marveled.

"Oliver tricked me into signing documents that would dissolve the trusts. The judge ruled that because it's been determined in a court of law that I'm insane, any legal documents I sign are invalid. Oliver has vowed I will die in here."

"Are you well?" Agatha asked.

"I know I'm dreadfully thin. But, yes, I'm well. My efforts to alter my dresses are being thwarted." She lifted the skirt of her dress and dropped it again.

"Do you need thread?" Agatha asked.

"No, thank you. I have threads aplenty. My sewing needles have disappeared. I have no idea who took them."

"We'll purchase some and give them to Beulah, along with some food," Agatha offered.

"Thank you. Food seems to disappear in the ward. I've not been able to discern who is taking it." Elizabeth shuddered.

"Are you chilled?" I asked.

"Yes. My shawl was missing this morning."

Mrs. Davidson approached. "Mrs. Ziegler, it's time to go back inside."

Disappointment showed on all our faces.

"We will be back next Saturday," I promised, then looked at Mrs. Davidson and asked, "Same time?"

"Yes." She grasped Elizabeth's arm. "It's nearly dinner time." She turned to Agatha and me. "It was very nice to make your acquaintance."

We watched Elizabeth and Mrs. Davidson return to the hospital, then made our way back to the open gate and the streetcar.

Chapter 29

15 April 1868

Several letters lay on the table in the foyer. Two were addressed to me—one from Melissa Brandt. I hadn't heard from her since January and prayed this letter would be the cheerful, newsy letter she had promised.

My heart leapt when I saw the other letter was from Bartholomew.

I rushed upstairs and divested myself of my satchel and outerwear before sitting on the edge of the bed to read Melissa's missive.

Her careful penmanship filled ten sheets of notepaper, chronicling her life since I left Norwich.

Why does she not mention Rachel? I wondered but reveled in the news from my childhood friend.

After reading her letter, I went downstairs and brought back a pot of tea and two sweet rolls. I poured a cup of tea, took a bite of a roll, and opened Bartholomew's letter.

Priscilla,

I am counting the days until you are able to come to Norwich. I yearn for the day I may once again gaze upon your beautiful face. I miss our long, meandering conversations.

The housekeeper and butler at Marian Morrison's house have been apprised of your visit. They are pleased you are the new owner but are anxious to know your plans for the house.

My parents have assured me you are welcome at Riverbend. They realize it was not your choice to leave your childhood home.

There are a few more documents for you to sign, and Mr. Osborne has set an appointment for you on Tuesday, 9 June, at 11 AM.

I will meet you at the Norwich train station and accompany you to Mrs. Morrison's—your—house.

I am
Your humble servant,
Bartholomew Martin

I sat holding the letter for some minutes before moving to the chair at the table and taking up pen and paper to respond, first to Bartholomew, then to Melissa.

Chapter 30

2 May 1868
Pennsylvania Hospital for the Insane
Philadelphia, Pennsylvania

Agatha and I sat on a bench, waiting for Elizabeth and Mrs. Davidson to come outside.

"Did you bring the notes for our meeting with Mr. Green?" I asked.

"Yes. I want to be certain we have the facts correct, and we ask appropriate questions."

"She may have questions we have not thought to ask," I indicated.

"Very true." Agatha paused as she saw women coming into the Ladies' Pleasure Ground. "Ah, there they are."

We stood and began to walk towards them.

"Good morning." Elizabeth smiled and touched the collar of her dress.

"I see you have made good use of the needles we sent." Agatha admired the better-fitting dress our friend wore.

"Thank you. I have learned to secrete one or two in my bed linen. Beulah keeps the remaining needles until I am in need of a new one." Elizabeth grasped Agatha's hand. "What news do you bring today?"

"We have an appointment to meet with an attorney willing to take your case. Mr. Green has successfully handled similar cases," I informed her. "We have some questions for you about your ordeal."

"It will take time, but we're confident Mr. Green will be able to have you declared sane and released."

Elizabeth's eyes sparkled with unshed tears. "I don't know what to say. Thank you."

We walked around a group of women patients and continued on the walking path past a small circular flower garden.

"Your mother, Dinah, and Gertrude all know we have seen you, and you are well."

Elizabeth's pace foundered, her face paled, her eyes widened, and she opened and closed her mouth. "You didn't say where I am, did you?"

Agatha moved to stand in front of her and grasped both hands. "Of course not. We don't want to risk your father or Oliver knowing we found you."

She pulled her hands free and placed one on her throat. "Thank heavens. I don't know what Oliver would do if he learned you've seen me."

Mrs. Davidson extended an arm to indicate our need to resume our stroll.

"Your family is worried about you, but everyone is well," I informed her. "Even Ruth believes Oliver has gone too far."

"Well, that's something," Elizabeth said. "You said you had some questions for me. What do you want to know?"

"Has Oliver ever hit you?" Agatha asked.

The bluntness of the question startled all of us, but Elizabeth quickly composed herself.

"Yes. Once. I told him if he ever laid hands on me again, I would leave his house and commence divorce proceedings. He scoffed at the remark but hasn't touched me since." She walked a few steps and continued. "He frequently attempted to belittle me by making remarks about the manner in which I kept house, the way my hair was dressed, or the manner of my speech. That sort of thing. He once remarked that if I was so unhappy, I could always shoot him like I did Percival Templeton."

"He didn't," I breathed in disbelief.

"He did," she confirmed. "I don't know how he learned about that or whether he knows the entire story. I have never spoken of anything that occurred in Texas to him or anyone else in Gettysburg."

We were no longer walking. Agatha and I stared at her with disbelief that Oliver Finch would think such a thing, much less speak it.

"It's time, Mrs. Ziegler," Mrs. Davidson said, coming to stand close beside me with her arms at her sides.

"Same time next week?" I asked.

She nodded and pressed something into my hand, then took a couple of steps away from me and towards Elizabeth.

As I looked down to see what it was, she moved her head slowly from side to side and placed a finger to her lips.

"Goodbye, Jeanne. We'll come again next week," Agatha said as we walked away.

Once outside the asylum gates, I unfolded the paper Mrs. Davidson had pressed into my hand.

"What do you have there?" Agatha asked.

"Mrs. Davidson gave this to me," I said, holding out the small piece of paper for us to read.

Meet me at the park on 48th Street in half an hour.

We exchanged looks, then turned towards Forty-eighth Street.

We followed Mrs. Davidson into the park. She led us to a secluded space within a small garden before turning to face us. "Thank you for coming. I want to assure you that Jeanne does not suffer from any mental disorder. I'm willing to help her in any way I can."

"We're uncertain how to help her," Agatha admitted. "You have heard that we have an appointment with a lawyer. Perhaps we'll know more about what we can do for her after we speak with him. We can most certainly include you in whatever plan we devise."

"Will aiding her jeopardize your job?" I asked.

"I will most certainly be discharged if I'm found out," she confirmed. "But, that is of little concern to me. The laws allowing husbands to condemn their wives to these places are inhumane. Those men are heartless. Many encourage their children to believe their mothers have abandoned them for a life of sin."

"That's horrible," I exclaimed. "Thank heavens Elizabeth—I mean Jeanne—has no children."

Church bells chimed the hour.

"I must go," Mrs. Davidson said. "I look forward to learning what the lawyer has to say." She walked away.

Agatha and I stared at her retreating back.

"Do you trust her?" I asked.

"I don't know. We should speak with Beulah."

We returned to town and ate a late dinner at a café before returning home.

After putting away my reticule, hat, and gloves, I entered the drawing room with my sewing basket, a book, and Bartholomew's most recent letter.

I chose a chair near a window facing the street. After reading the letter, I picked up the partially finished chemisette.

Chapter 31

13 May 1868
Law Office of Paul Green

Agatha, Beulah, and I nervously sat across from Mr. Green as he reviewed the documents we had presented to him.

He sat back in his chair and removed his glasses. "This is an interesting case. Mrs. Finch appears to be an exceptional woman. I'm curious to learn how she knew to appoint an unrelated man to control her affairs. It is not a point of law most married women know about."

"Mrs. Finch is quite remarkable," I confirmed. "Before her recent marriage to Oliver Finch, she was a widow and managed her own affairs. She taught war widows to do the same."

"You don't say," he marveled. "I shall look forward to speaking with her." He shuffled the papers on his desk. "You say she is currently at the state asylum here in Philadelphia?"

"Yes. Her husband forbids anyone except himself to visit her," Agatha explained.

"But we have found a way to circumvent that," I added. "We have been to see her every week since Holy Saturday."

"Do I want to know how you've managed that feat?"

"We meet outside on one of the Ladies' Pleasure Grounds," Agatha stated.

"There's more than one?" he asked.

"There is one at the front of the hospital and a larger

one behind it," Beulah explained. "The woman who accompanies her is sympathetic to the women in that ward and is willing to help Mrs. Finch."

"I see." He steepled his fingers and touched his index finger to his lips before placing his hands on the desk. "Would it be untoward for me to visit her?"

Agatha, Beulah, and I exchanged looks of surprise.

"No. No, I suspected you would want to speak with her. If anyone from the hospital asks, we can provide an explanation for your presence."

"It would be best to tell Mrs. Finch before you come," Agatha stated.

"Most certainly." He glanced at his notes. "You say you visit her every Saturday?"

"Yes. We take the streetcar," Agatha informed him.

"And, you'll be going next Saturday?" he asked.

We nodded.

He studied a calendar that hung on the wall next to his desk. "Please inform Mrs. Finch that I will accompany you on your visit in two weeks."

I sat a bit straighter and smiled. "May I infer you are accepting her as a client?"

"You may." He stood and moved around the side of the desk to open his office door for us. "Thank you for coming in, ladies. I shall see you on the streetcar in two weeks."

We rose and left.

I felt giddy and fought the urge to hug the gentleman.

Chapter 32

29 May 1868
Pennsylvania Hospital for the Insane

Paul Green, Esquire, boarded the streetcar two stops after Agatha and me. He nodded as he passed us to take a vacant seat three rows behind. We were the only passengers to disembark at the stand near the hospital.

"I don't recall seeing any men on the Ladies' Pleasure Grounds," Agatha observed as we crossed under the arched entrance to the hospital.

"Perhaps the men visit indoors," I suggested.

"I doubt many men come to visit their female relations in this place," Mr. Green stated.

"That is most likely the truth of the matter," I said.

We were crossing the path leading to the large double doors to the building.

"Have you visited anyone here, Mr. Green?" I asked.

"I have represented women who were in the same situation as Mrs. Finch," he replied.

"Were you able to help them?" Agatha enquired.

"There have been five ladies. Two died under circumstances that were never satisfactorily explained. Three have been adjudged sane and released from this place."

"Did their husbands accept them back?" Agatha asked.

"One gentleman repented his actions and accepted his wife back into their home with open arms. Two others wanted nothing more to do with their wives. One lady now lives with her adult son and his family. The other now lives in another state."

Mr. Green looked at the farmland on our right and the Ladies' Pleasure Ground to our left. Turning the corner of the hospital and following the walking path to the rear, Mr. Green stopped and took in our surroundings. "I've never been back here." Pointing to two buildings in the distance, he asked, "What are those buildings to the right, near the perimeter wall?"

"I do not know," I replied. "We should ask Mrs. Davidson."

"Who is Mrs. Davidson?" he asked.

"She is the hospital employee who attends to Elizabeth when she is outside," Agatha explained.

"Of course. I believe you spoke of her when you were in my office."

"Look," Agatha exclaimed, pointing towards an open door at the back of the hospital. "The ladies are coming outside."

We stood still, watching the women and their attendants move through the doorway and into the sunshine.

"There is Elizabeth," I proclaimed and waved at my friend.

Elizabeth hugged Agatha and me, then looked curiously at Mr. Green.

Agatha introduced him to Elizabeth and Mrs. Davidson.

"I'm pleased to make your acquaintance, Mr. Green. Please take care to address our patient as Jeanne Zigler. She was admitted as a patient under that name," Mrs. Davidson cautioned.

Mr. Green nodded. "Thank you. I shall keep that in mind." He turned to Elizabeth. I am pleased to meet you, Mrs. Ziegler. I've spoken at length with Miss Llewellyn and Miss Bentley. I'd like to hear your story in your own words."

"My first husband died in a mining accident in California. He owned a half-interest in a gold mine, had substantial sums in a bank in San Francisco, and other assets. It all passed to me through his will. His mining partner bought out my share of the mine, which added to my wealth.

"My father believes me to be headstrong and frivolous. He is convinced I'm incapable of managing my affairs. Because I was an unmarried woman when I returned to Gettysburg last year, he could only berate me. After a great deal of thought, I am convinced he and my husband conspired to take control of my assets. The judge who declared me insane is an old friend of my father.

"Oliver became enraged when he learned all my valuable possessions had been placed in several trusts. I named my attorney, Mr. David McConaughy, as trustee. The beneficiaries of these trusts are my niece, nephew, and myself. I received a monthly stipend from one of the trusts, which was suspended when I was declared insane.

"After the court hearing, I was taken to Pennsylvania Hospital for the Insane in Harrisburg, using my true name, Elizabeth Finch. I was there a month or two before Oliver sent two thuggish men to bring me here, and I was admitted under the name Jeanne Ziegler." She wiped a tear from her eye as she finished.

Mr. Green looked up from the notes he'd been writing. "How did you know to establish the trusts?"

"Before I married Oliver, I worked with war widows to help them establish their independence from supposedly well-meaning male relatives. I learned that married women are permitted by law to make business decisions while their husbands are living but are absent from the home. Most of my clients managed the family farm or business while their husbands served in the army or navy without interference.

"I also learned about placing assets in trusts with a non-relative as trustee as a method of protecting a woman's separate property, whether owned prior to the marriage or inherited during the marriage.

"Most of these men died without wills but left young, underaged sons to inherit their estates. Their unscrupulous male relations swoop in and declare themselves guardians of these young boys without the benefit of being appointed such in a court of law. Some even tried this when there was a will leaving the estate to their wives."

Mr. Green wrote furiously, glancing up now and again with admiration. "Has he tried to break your trusts?"

"Yes. The days flow together, and I don't recall how long ago, but he came here to see me and demanded that I sign a document he wouldn't allow me to read. I later learned it was a petition to dissolve the trusts. It was denied because I had been determined to be insane prior to the date of the petition."

"Did anyone else see you sign that document?" he asked.

"I did," Mrs. Davidson responded. "It is hospital policy that an attendant accompany patients when they have visitors. I witnessed her signing what appeared to be a legal document."

Mr. Green turned his attention to Mrs. Davidson. "Did he speak with you while he was visiting?"

"Yes. He threatened to disfigure my face should I tell anyone he came to see Mrs. Ziegler." She shook her head. "He's a very unpleasant man. I didn't hear what was said, but Mrs. Ziegler told him something, and he struck her, knocking her to the floor. An orderly who happened to be nearby restrained Mr. Ziegler, as he called himself. A matron instructed the orderly to escort Mr. Ziegler from the building. As he was being led out, he shouted that Mrs. Ziegler would die here."

Agatha and I gasped, and we each took one of Elizabeth's hands.

Mr. Green wrote quickly, then looked up from his notes. "Thank you, Mrs. Davidson. Would you be willing to testify to this in court?"

"Most assuredly. Most of the women on that ward should not be there," she asserted. "The diagnosis of 'female hysteria' is laughable. It's a means for men to be rid of their wives without the stigma of divorce."

Mr. Green stared at Mrs. Davidson, eyebrows raised and mouth forming an 'O'.

"Do you really believe that?" Agatha asked.

"I certainly do. The women on this ward are as sane as we are. Their husbands became displeased with them for frivolous reasons. So, they found a doctor who would give the diagnosis they needed to send their wives here or some other institution." Mrs. Davidson gasped for breath.

"You feel quite strongly about this," I observed quietly.

"She is correct," Mr. Green confirmed.

Elizabeth nodded. "Most of us have been given the diagnosis of 'female hysteria.'"

Will you be able to engage a doctor who will certify Elizabeth's sanity?" I asked.

Mrs. Davidson glared at me as I realized I had used her true name. "It's time Mrs. Ziegler returned to the ward."

"I shall contact the doctor I previously consulted. We will speak again soon," Mr. Green said as he pushed papers into his satchel.

"Goodbye, Jeanne. We'll see you next week." Agatha

hugged her and stepped back.

"Please use my true name. I prefer it to the alias I've been forced to use here," Elizabeth said.

"We shall," I promised. "Goodbye, Elizabeth. Take care of yourself."

Mr. Green, Agatha, and I watched them start across the Ladies' Pleasure Grounds.

"One last question, if I may?" Mr. Green called and pointed to the small buildings to our right. "What are those buildings?"

"They're the laundry," Mrs. Davidson replied over her shoulder as she continued guiding Elizabeth toward the door.

"Hmmm," he said under his breath as we retraced our steps to the streetcar stand.

Chapter 33

6 June 1868

The spring school term ended on 5 June. Agatha and I marked exam papers into the early morning hours. Nevertheless, we were on the streetcar by ten o'clock to visit Elizabeth before we left Philadelphia.

Elizabeth and Mrs. Davidson were already outside when we arrived.

"I was afraid you'd already gone home," Elizabeth proclaimed when she saw us.

"We could not leave without seeing you," I replied.

"When do you depart?" Mrs. Davidson asked.

"Monday morning," Agatha replied. "I'll be returning to Philadelphia on 6 July.

And what about you, Priscilla?" When do you travel to Norwich?" Elizabeth enquired.

"The train leaves for New York at 11 AM Monday," I explained. "I plan to remain in Norwich for two or three weeks."

We followed the walking path near the hospital perimeter and past the laundry buildings situated south and east of the main building.

"Have you news from Mr. Green?" Agatha asked.

"Yes. The doctor Mr. Green consulted for the previous cases passed away two years ago. He's speaking with doctors who may be willing to declare I have regained my senses and am ready to return to society," Elizabeth reported. "As soon as a doctor certifies me sane, Mr. Green will file the petition."

"I pray he is able to engage someone soon," I said.

"I'm sorry," Mrs. Davidson interrupted. "It's time Mrs. Ziegler went back inside." She grasped my left hand, and I felt something being pressed into my palm. "Safe travels to you both."

"Please keep her well," Agatha implored.

"I shall do my best," Mrs. Davidson vowed as she touched Elizabeth's elbow and guided her back to the hospital.

Agatha and I watched them until they were inside, then turned to retrace our steps. As we walked by the laundry, I noticed a door in the perimeter wall.

"Agatha, look," I said, pointing to the door.

She reached out, tried the latch, and turned slightly to face me. "It's unlocked." She opened the door wide enough for us to cross the threshold, then shut it tightly.

"Do you suppose we were meant to discover this door?" Agatha asked as we stood in the street outside the asylum grounds.

"I am unsure. She handed me something before they went inside." I opened my left hand to reveal a tightly folded paper.

"Open it," Agatha instructed.

I removed my gloves to more easily unfold the paper. Mrs. Davidson's compact writing filled the small note paper.

What is it?' Agatha asked.

"Mrs. Davidson's home address. She asks that we write to her while we are away."

"I'll copy it into my address book this evening," Agatha

116

professed.

We were discussing Agatha's impending visit with Dinah Hoffman, Elizabeth's sister, when we entered the foyer of the rooming house.

"Miss Llewellyn, you have a visitor in the sitting room," Faith, Mrs. Peele's elder daughter, announced as she exited the dining room. "He's been here for more than an hour."

"Thank you, Faith." I turned into the sitting room while removing my gloves.

"Good afternoon, Priscilla," Bartholomew Martin rose from a chair as he greeted me.

"Bartholomew, what a pleasant surprise. I didn't expect to see you until Tuesday," I said, moving further into the room.

"I was sitting in my flat last evening when it occurred to me that you would be traveling unescorted. I quickly packed a bag and caught the early morning train."

"I'm sorry I wasn't here when you arrived. Agatha and I went to visit a friend."

"It is of no matter. I took a room at a hotel, washed off the soot from the train, and then came here. I hadn't foreseen you would likely be visiting your friend this morning."

"It is very thoughtful of you to escort me to Norwich. I considered having a traveling companion but decided to travel alone." I sat across from Bartholomew and studied him. He was taller than me and had sandy blond hair. His eyes were the color of cornflowers. "And how is everyone in Norwich?"

"About the same as before you traveled to Texas."

"Except Aunt Marian is no longer nestled on her divan in her private sitting room."

"Yes, except for that."

I placed my gloves and reticule on the side table and allowed my shawl to fall from my shoulders.

"Melissa Brandt is excited about your visit."

"I pray she has forgiven my failure to maintain correspondence with her. I vowed to never return to Norwich. I thought there was nothing for me there." I sat quietly for a moment. "It is amazing what can occur in two years."

"You have implied there were many adventures," he stated quietly.

"I suppose they could be called adventures, but I don't think of them as such. Mr. Pennyman was a ruthless man who surrounded himself with like-minded men.

"The sister and brother of one of those men pursued me from Texas to Massachusetts and tried to kill me." I paused, then added, "Those people met their fates. Elizabeth was married in April, and I came here to teach. We were both content with our new beginnings when her husband had her legally confined to an asylum."

"I remember hearing my father speak disapprovingly of your father's business arrangement with Josiah Pennyman. It seems most men in Norwich didn't trust him. I assumed it was because he was a Southerner."

"I never understood why Papa arranged the marriage. I met Josiah Pennyman for the first time when I arrived at his home in Texas." I hesitated a moment. "Did you know James Kilpatrick is practicing law in Corpus Christi?"

"No, I didn't. James and my older brother, Enoc, were friends. They were at school together."

"Papa and I attended Enoc's wedding." Again, there was a lapse in the conversation. "Papa had certain legal documents sent to James. I presume Mr. Osborne was involved in that."

"I've not had reason to work on your father's files," Bartholomew said. "You and your father left Norwich before I went to work in Mr. Osborne's office."

"It was a pleasant surprise the first time I saw James in Texas. He helped me a great deal. In fact, he continues to handle certain legal matters for me."

"I wonder whether Mr. Osborne knows that," he mused. "You should probably mention it when you see Mr. Osborne next week."

"I will."

Movement in the foyer caught my attention as I heard a clock chime seven.

"Oh, my. I had no idea of the hour. Dinner is being served." I stood and gathered my things to take upstairs.

"Mrs. Peele invited me to join you. I'll wait for you in the foyer," he said, walking behind me as I made for the stairs.

Miss Adams looked up when we entered the dining room. I took my usual place, with Bartholomew on my right and Agatha to my left.

"What is this world coming to? A man at our table," Miss Adams spat before I could make introductions.

"Mr. Martin is an attorney. He came to Philadelphia to escort me to Norwich," I explained rather feebly.

With a dour look from me to Bartholomew, Miss Adams quipped, "So, you once again bring disgrace to Mrs. Peele's doorstep."

"No, she doesn't," Bartholomew patiently explained. "I represent Miss Llewellyn's late godmother."

Incredulity was writ on Miss Adams' face. "I beg your pardon. I didn't know."

"It's a pleasure to see you again," Beulah commented. "We met briefly when you were here last winter."

"I ought to introduce everyone," I said. "You remember Miss Beulah Snodgrass and Miss Agatha Bentley. The lady to Beulah's right is Miss Daphne Crane, and to her right is Miss Barbara Adams. Ladies', this gentleman is Mr. Bartholomew Martin, an attorney from Norwich, Connecticut."

"I'm honored to meet all of you," he responded.

"I'm relieved Priscilla won't be traveling alone," Agatha said.

"May I escort you ladies to church tomorrow morning?" Bartholomew asked.

"That would be wonderful," Agatha replied.

"I can join you if you attend an early service," Beulah observed. "I must be at the hospital at noon."

"Would the eight o'clock service be too early?" I asked.

Miss Adams remained silent, wearing a slight scowl.

"May I join you?" Miss Crane asked in a very soft voice.

"Of course," I replied. "Everyone is welcome in the Lord's house. Miss Adams, would you care to join us?"

"I'll stay home, thank you," she replied without looking up from her empty plate.

"We shall be ready at seven thirty," I announced.

"Thank you for a lovely meal, Mrs. Peele," Bartholomew said as he prepared to return to his hotel.

"You are most welcome. Please break your fast with us when you return from services," the landlady responded.

"Thank you for the invitation. Good night." Bartholomew turned to me. "I'll see you in the morning."

"We will all be ready. Good night."

He was walking into the twilight when I shut the door.

Chapter 34

7 June 1868

I heard voices in the dining room when I came downstairs to wait for Bartholomew. I stood at the foot of the stairs to listen.

"You're acting like a schoolgirl," Miss Adams complained.

"I'm attending church with women I consider friends," countered Miss Crane.

"I can't imagine why. They're three decades younger than you."

"Age has nothing to do with it. They're very nice young women whose company I enjoy."

"You've not stepped foot in a church in twenty years," Miss Adams pointed out.

"I've been remiss in tending to my spiritual needs. I mean to correct that."

"Why today? Is it that Mr. Martin?" Miss Adams spat.

"He's smitten with Miss Llewellyn," Miss Crane declared.

I gasped and held my right hand to my mouth. *Is it true? Oh, please let it be true.* I quietly moved from the foyer to the drawing room and took a chair.

Several minutes passed before Miss Crane came in and took a position near me. "I'm sorry about Barbara."

You need not apologize for her."

"She's much too vocal with her opinions and suppositions."

"I will not disagree. I suppose she means well."

"Not always," Miss Crane shook her head. "I sometimes think she thrives on the controversy."

"Was she very upset with Mr. Morton having supper with us?"

"No, not at all. She enjoys dissension—as long as it doesn't involve her directly. Now, enough about Barbara. What about you? Are you ready to return to Norwich?"

I reflected on that question. "I do not know what to expect. Will my friends forgive my extended silence? Should I tell them everything that has occurred since I was last with them?"

"And what about returning to your childhood home?"

"It is no longer my home. Papa sold it to Bartholomew's father." I felt tears welling.

Miss Crane reached out and touched my hand. "Where will you stay?"

"I inherited my godmother's house. I'll stay there."

Miss Crane's face brightened. "How lovely. I'm delighted for you."

"Truth be told, I'm nervous about being there as well. I never knew my mother, and I spent a good deal of time at Aunt Marian's. There are so many memories..."

"Oh, my dear girl, I pray the memories are happy, and you will rejoice in your godmother's love."

"Most of my memories of her and her house are wonderful. I miss Aunt Marian so much."

"I know. I've lost people, too. Remember all the wonderful moments—even the small ones. Your Aunt Marian is in every nook and cranny of that house. I pray you are embraced by her love when you enter it."

"Thank you, Miss Crane. I have thought only of the emptiness of the house. I shall endeavor to recall the happy moments."

"Yes, there will be a sense of emptiness, especially in her room. But, your Aunt Marian's essence remains."

Agatha entered, breaking the moment.

I brushed away the tears and squeezed Miss Crane's hand. "Thank you," I whispered to her.

"Beulah will be down in a minute," Agatha stated, then looked from Miss Crane to me. "Did I interrupt something?"

"No, no. We were talking of Miss Llewellyn's trip to Norwich," Miss Crane explained.

I heard footfalls on the stairs just before the doorbell rang.

"I'll get it," Beulah called from the bottom step. I heard the door open and close.

Bartholomew followed her into the drawing room. "Good morning, ladies. There's a bit of a drizzle this morning, so I took the liberty of hiring a carriage for all of us,"

"That was very thoughtful of you, Mr. Martin," Miss Crane said.

She and I rose from our chairs, smiled at one another, and followed the others outside and into the large carriage for the brief journey to Christ Church.

Upon our return to the boardinghouse after church, Mrs. Peele and her daughters served a lavish brunch, which even Miss Adams enjoyed.

Calah returned from spending Shabbot with her family and joined us in the dining room.

After brunch, Beulah went upstairs and donned her work clothes. She came back downstairs and sought us out. "Thank you, Mr. Martin. The carriage rides were most enjoyable. Safe travels to you both. Let's not lose touch while you're gone. You will be missed."

"We'll miss all of you as well," Agatha returned. And hugged our friend.

"Do watch out for our mutual friend," I added as I embraced her.

"I shall."

"The streetcars don't run on Sundays. How are you getting to the hospital?" I asked.

"I will take a cab," Beulha replied matter-of-factly.

"Nonsense," Bartholomew said. "Priscilla and I are going for a drive. I'll have the driver take you to the asylum."

I raised my eyebrows at his declaration. "I'll get my things," I said and dashed upstairs, holding the front of my skirt above my ankles to avoid tripping.

The rain had stopped when we stepped outside and made our way to the waiting carriage. The three of us were soon settled into the carriage and were on our way to Pennsylvania Hospital for the Insane.

The drive was pleasant. We traveled through parts of the city I had never seen, some quite appalling, while others were picturesque. In much less time than when we traveled by streetcar, we were at the gates of the asylum.

Always a gentleman, Bartholomew stepped out and assisted Beulah to disembark.

"How will you return home?" I asked.

"One of the other cleaners has a dog cart. I will get a ride with her," Beulah nodded to Bartholomew. "Thank you so much, Mr. Martin. I hope to see you again." She turned and followed the walking path to the front doors of the hospital.

Bartholomew resumed his seat next to me. "Where to, Miss Llewellyn?"

"Fairmount Park is a lovely locale for a carriage ride," I replied.

"Fairmount Park, if you please, driver," he instructed.

The driver slowed the horses' pace to travel the tree-lined lanes inside the park. Bartholomew asked the driver to stop when we came upon the Schuylkill River, and we stepped out of the carriage.

"How many times have I strolled the riverbank at home?" I asked as we strolled alongside the river.

"Too many to count, I dare say," Bartholomew replied. "Though, I much preferred reposing in the stand of trees along the riverbank."

"I enjoyed many picnics under those trees and read many books. My French tutor would take me there. She thought being outdoors was more conducive to learning."

"Lucky you." He smiled.

"It was far more pleasant conjugating French verbs in the shade of those trees than in a stuffy school room on the second floor."

He chuckled. "I suppose it would be."

We walked a bit further before he asked, "Do you want to visit Riverbend?"

I stopped walking, uncertain how to reply. Of course, I yearned to return to my childhood home, the place of my ancestors. But it was no longer my home. "I don't know, Bartholomew. How would your mother feel about me being there?"

"You would be welcomed with open arms. The house is unchanged."

"Let me think about it. I do want to visit the mausoleum. My mother is there."

"I've been there many times since Father bought the

farm. It's a wonderful place to ponder weighty matters. And your great-grandfather is a wonderful listener."

"Papa used to go there to talk to Mama. I best get back and finish packing. It's getting late."

He signaled the driver who brought the carriage to us.

Agatha and I had finished packing, leaving out only those items required for our evening and morning ablutions. After supper, we moved to the drawing room.

"You ladies are certainly quiet this evening," Miss Crane observed as she came in and claimed a chair near us.

"There is much to ponder and little to say," I remarked.

"Yes, going home is always difficult," Miss Crane noted. "I've not been home in, oh my, forty-five years now."

"What brought you to the United States?"

"I came to be married to a distant cousin. Unfortunately, he died before my ship made port in New York, and I didn't have the funds to make the return trip."

"How did you meet Miss Adams?" Agatha enquired.

"She's the sister of my betrothed. She was much lighter-hearted in those days. Life has made her quite cynical. "

"I would have liked to have known the younger Miss Adams," Agatha said.

"What about you, Miss Crane?" You're usually very quiet and allow Miss Adams to run roughshod over you."

"I find it easier to let her have her way. But, you ladies have given me the strength to speak for myself. Barbara is not pleased with this turn of events."

A grin broke across my face. "Well done, Miss Crane. It's always best to speak for yourself."

A clock chimed nine thirty.

"It's getting late, and I have an early train to Harrisburg," Agatha announced, rising from her chair.

"Should I not see you on the morrow, I bid you farewell." She glided towards the foyer.

"I pray you have an enjoyable visit with your family," offered Miss Crane.

"I shall also bid you all good night." I followed my friend to the door.

"I believe I shall also retire," Miss Crane declared as she stood and walked with me to the second floor. "There's no reason for me to sit here alone."

Chapter 35

8 June 1868

Bartholomew and I arrived at the Reading Railroad Station thirty minutes before the train to New York was to depart. After checking my trunk through to Norwich, we found the correct platform and waited for the train to arrive.

Once on the train, we selected seats away from the windows and settled down to read as the conveyance left Philadelphia.

We arrived in New York with little time to spare before boarding the train to New Haven. The closer we drew to Norwich, the more apprehensive I became. I could no longer concentrate on reading. The book lay open on my lap.

"Are you well?" Bartholomew asked.

"I am having second thoughts about returning to Norwich. It is almost as though I am skulking into town."

"Your friends know you're returning for a visit," he assured me.

"How do they know?" I asked.

"These things have a way of getting out," he replied cryptically.

After a brief stopover in New Haven, we were on our way to

Norwich.

Bartholomew gently laid his hand over mine. "You're trembling. There's nothing to be nervous about. You will be surrounded by friends. I arranged for your carriage to be at the station."

I stepped off the train into the afternoon sunshine and drew deep breaths. The scents of the city clinging to the air were as familiar as the clothes I wore. "I am in Norwich," I uttered.

"Yes, you are," Bartholomew said and offered his arm.

"Would you mind walking rather than using the carriage?" I asked.

Confusion clouded his otherwise good looks.

"We have been sitting for hours," I explained, "and I would like to look at the city."

"All right," he said. "I'll speak to your driver."

"No, I will do it," I said firmly, marching purposefully toward the gleaming maroon carriage.

The footman moved to open the door.

"No need, Yancy. I have decided to walk. You and Kloth may return home after you have collected my trunk." I handed him my carpet bag and the baggage claim ticket.

"Yes, ma'am." He nodded, put the carpetbag inside, and spoke to Kloth, my driver.

Bartholomew and I watched them strap my trunk to the carriage and move towards Aunt Marian's house.

"Where to, m'lady?" he asked.

"This way." I turned and began walking.

The tree-lined streets were both familiar and strange. I recognized the homes of people with whom I was acquainted before I traveled to Texas.

"What will people say when they learn I did not marry Josiah Pennyman? Will they think me a fallen woman?" I

asked.

He did not respond immediately. "The people close to you will know the truth." Bartholomew glanced at me and reached across himself to squeeze my hand resting on his coat sleeve. "Others may privately speculate but will never say anything publicly. There will always be those who think and believe the worst."

"I suppose."

We turned a corner and crossed a street.

"Will you stay for supper?" I asked. "I don't want to be alone." I looked at him with pleading in my eyes.

"What have you to be nervous about?" You have stayed in that house countless times."

"But I was never alone. Aunt Marian was always there." We walked a half-block before I continued. "What is it like to live completely alone, with no family or servants or anyone else?"

The corners of his lips turned up. "Very quiet."

"I have never lived alone," I confessed.

"And you won't be now. You have household staff."

"From my experience, it is not the same. I cannot sit down for a meal with them. With the exception of my lady's maid, they cannot accompany me to any entertainment."

"True. I'm certain Melissa Brandt will be a willing companion."

I glanced up and abruptly stopped walking. There it was in front of me—Aunt Marian's house—my house. I tightened my grasp on his arm. "It is so large," I murmured. I was nearly overwhelmed with sadness as I realized that Aunt Marian was not inside, awaiting my arrival.

He wrinkled his brow. "What?"

"Do you not feel the emptiness? Aunt Marian is not here." I was overwhelmed with sadness.

"I suppose it's much the way I felt the first time I went

inside the manor at Riverbend after you and your father left. It looked the same. All the furniture was exactly where it had always been. It was unsettling to be in that house, as though I was somewhere I ought not to be."

The door opened as we walked up the path and over the threshold into the foyer.

I fought to maintain my composure as Ulbrect Wilson, my godmother's butler—my butler—shut the door and took Bartholomew's hat.

"Welcome home, Miss Llewellyn," Wilson greeted. "Mrs. Ingram had your room prepared."

"The room I previously occupied or Aunt Marian's rooms?"

"The room you traditionally occupy, ma'am," he confirmed. "Mrs. Morrison's rooms have not been disturbed."

"Thank you."

"Do you wish to address the staff, Miss Llewellyn?"

"I hadn't thought of that. I suppose I ought to, but it can wait till tomorrow."

"Yes, ma'am. And, what time do you wish supper to be served? Mrs. Reese will want to know."

"I am accustomed to dining at seven. Please tell Mrs. Reese I do not require a separate meal from what she prepares for the staff. It is wasteful to prepare two distinct meals unless we have guests."

"Yes, ma'am," A wary look crossed Wilson's face. "I shall deliver the message. Is there anything else you require?"

"No, not a thing. Thank you, Wilson."

He bowed and backed out of the room, leaving Bartholomew and me alone.

"Shall we go to the library?"

Our footfalls echoed on the wooden floor.

The library was filled with the faint fragrance of ink, paper, and old leather. The curtains were open, allowing afternoon sunlight to flood the room. Aunt Marian's favorite chair was directly in front of the fireplace. The book she had been reading lay open on the side table.

I walked around the room, looking at each knickknack and occasionally reading the titles printed on the spines of the books on the shelves.

"This is quite a large collection," Bartholomew observed as he pulled down a book and perused its contents. He replaced the book and continued to inspect the shelves. "I suppose I ought to leave. I must be in court tomorrow morning but should return to the office before your appointment."

"I cannot entice you to stay for supper?"

"I'm sorry, no."

I tugged on the bell pull and walked with him to the foyer. "Thank you for escorting me here." I touched the sleeve of his coat.

"My pleasure."

Wilson came in, carrying Bartholomew's hat.

"Thank you, Wilson," he said.

The butler nodded and opened the door.

"Good night, Mr. Martin," I offered and made my way back to the library.

After supper, I remained downstairs, delaying having to pass the door to Aunt Marian's rooms.

Her private sitting room was adjacent to her bed chamber and was the last place I saw her before I left Norwich—and where she breathed her last breath. I wasn't ready to not find her there.

I sat with my feet on the small sofa and closed my eyes. I was unused to being as utterly alone as I was at that moment when I felt something land heavily on my lower limbs. I opened my eyes to see a caramel-colored cat staring at me. She walked slowly up my skirt until her face was nearly touching my nose.

"Well, hello, Peanut. I have been away a very long time." I timidly touched her head. "Do you remember me?"

She moved in a tight circle twice before lying on my lap and purred.

It was well past eleven when I steeled my nerves and mounted the stairs to the second floor. As I made my way down the hall to my room, I sent up a prayer of thanks that the door to Aunt Marian's rooms was closed.

When I entered, Julie Norris, Aunt Marian's lady's maid, was putting away my clothes.

"Good evening, Miss Llewellyn. I'm nearly finished here. Would you like to prepare for bed?"

"Hello, Norris. How have you been?" I asked.

"It's been difficult with Mrs. Morrison gone, but I've taken the time to tidy her rooms and tend to her clothing that required attention."

"Bless you. I haven't the mettle to open that door." I removed my shoes and began unfastening my dress as we spoke. "I must warn you, I have been without a lady's maid these past two years and have become quite accustomed to doing for myself."

"I will understand if you wish to dismiss me," she said, picking up the dress and underpinnings I left on the floor.

I looked up from unfastening the busk on my corset. "I have no intention of dismissing anyone. My wardrobe is in sore need of a practiced eye. Two dresses were damaged beyond repair. My petticoats have holes in them, which I inexpertly patched. I've not had new underpinnings since I left Norwich, with the exception of the drawers and chemise I sewed last winter."

She handed a nightdress to me. "I will take a closer look at all your underpinnings, including the petticoats. We'll have your wardrobe restored before the summer is over."

I let the nightdress drop over my head and fastened the buttons at the neck. "I shall retire now. Good night, Norris."

"Good night, Miss Llewellyn. It's nice to have you here." Norris left, shutting the door behind her.

I turned down the wick of the lamp on my bedside table and settled into bed. I fell asleep shortly after laying my head on the pillow.

Chapter 36

9 June 1868
Norwich, Connecticut

I woke early, rose, and began to dress.

Norris quietly opened the door and stepped into the room. "Oh, Miss Llewellyn, you should have called for me."

I poked my head and arms through the petticoat and settled it over my crinoline. "I am afraid I did not think about calling for you. I will try to remember tomorrow."

"What would you like for breakfast?" Norris asked.

"Whatever Mrs. Reese has prepared for the staff will be fine. I am not finicky about what is on my plate."

"Tea or coffee?"

"Tea, please. I have never acquired a taste for coffee."

"I'll go down and inform Mrs. Reese, then come back and dress your hair."

"Oh, also, tell Mrs. Reese and Wilson I will likely not be home for dinner. I plan to pay a call after I have seen Mr. Osborne at eleven." I fastened the waistband on the petticoat, then stepped to the writing table and picked up an envelope. "And, have this delivered to the Brandt home."

I'll return in five minutes." Norris took the message and dashed out of the room. I heard the door to the back staircase close and donned my dress before sitting at the dressing table to brush out my hair and await her return.

Stepping outside the house, I paused to look at the lush greenery up and down the street. *The gardens are so beautiful. It is a pity I never gave them a second thought before I went to Texas.* The gentle breeze carried the scent of various flowers. I negotiated the steps and walkway to the street, then turned towards Mr. Osborne's office.

As I strolled on the boardwalks of the business district, I noted most of the shops were the same, though there was a new millinery shop. I promised myself I would explore it in the near future.

I arrived at Mr. Osborne's office fifteen minutes early and sat quietly while I waited. Bartholomew came in carrying a large case. "Good morning, Miss Llewellyn. " He nodded to me, then turned his attention to the law clerk. "Arnold, the Bauer case has been set for a ten-day trial beginning September seventeenth at ten o'clock. Please see that it's on the calendar."

"Yes, Mr. Martin. I'll do it right now."

Bartholomew disappeared behind a door, and I continued to wait.

An older man entered and announced he had an appointment with Mr. Osborne at the same hour as my appointment.

I started to say something about it when Mr. Osborne appeared at the same door Bartholomew had used and invited the gentleman and me into his office.

Introductions were made, and I learned the older gentleman was Mr. William Forsythe, Papa's financial agent and friend.

As soon as I heard his name, I recalled meeting him in 1865 when he dined at Riverbend. He had asked many peculiar questions about my youthful exploits. *I wonder whether that had anything to do with Josiah Pennyman.*

I was handed several documents as Mr. Osborne informed me that Mr. Forsythe and he worked with James Kilpatrick in Corpus Christi and the attorney in Houston handling Josiah Pennyman's probate to resolve the issues relating to the business in which Papa had invested. Fifty percent of the proceeds from sales to the Union were deposited into a new bank account in my name. The other fifty percent was added to Pennyman's estate.

"What happened to the funds from the Confederate sales?" I asked. "I must confess I used a portion of those funds to reimburse a family whose farm was damaged by Josiah's men and to repair Mr. Kilpatrick's buggy, which was damaged in the same incident."

"Your generosity was acknowledged and was but a small amount of the proceeds from those sales. Those funds were also divided. There are groups helping the families of the war dead. Half was awarded to groups in the north, with the other half distributed to groups in the south."

"I like that. I have an acquaintance in Gettysburg who works with war widows to help them maintain their independence from their male relatives who wish to control their lives."

"As unmarried women, that is their right," Mr. Osborne observed, then handed me another document. "This is related to your godmother, Marian Morrison."

"Is it not settled?" I asked.

"Yes, it is. While the investments were in probate and under my control, I consulted with Mr. Forsythe. I arranged for Mrs. Morrison's bank accounts and investments to be transferred into your name," Mr. Osborne explained.

"I would advise you to divest yourself of some of those investments," Mr. Forsythe added.

"I would be interested to hear what you have to say, but not today. Perhaps we may meet next week when I am more settled."

"That would be fine. I can call on you if you would prefer not to go to my office."

"I would prefer to meet at your office.

"Would Wednesday next week at ten be too early?"

"No. That would be fine."

"You must go to the bank today and sign documents for Mr. Brandt," Mr. Forsythe added.

"Thank you," I said. "I will go to the bank when I leave here."

Mr. Osborne shuffled papers together and placed them in a folder. "You are comfortably well off, Miss Llewellyn. There is no need for you to return to teaching."

The two men stood.

"I do not teach because I need to earn a wage. I teach because I want to fill my days with purpose." I stated, also rising.

The men stood still and stared at me.

"You are a remarkable young woman," uttered Mr. Forsythe. "Your father would be very proud."

I went directly to the bank owned by Mr. Henry Brandt, one of Papa's oldest friends and father of one of my closest friends.
I approached a teller. "I am Miss Priscilla Llewellyn. I am here to see Mr. Henry Brandt."

"He's expecting you. One moment, please," the teller explained before stepping away.

"Priscilla, how wonderful to see you again. Grace and Melissa are beside themselves with excitement at your return," Mr. Brandt said.

"Good morning, Mr. Brandt. I am relieved to know I am still welcome in your home."

"You shall always have a place in our home. There are a few documents you must sign, and then you will have access to your new bank accounts." He pushed an envelope across the desk." These are letters of introduction and credit for your use."

"Thank you. I opened a bank account in Philadelphia with my first wage packet from the school district."

"I did not know you sought employment," he remarked, pushing several papers across his desk with an ink pot and pen.

I signed where indicated and left the papers and writing instrument on the desk.

"What are your plans for the remainder of the day?" he enquired.

"I am going to pay a call on your wife and daughter."

Mr. Brandt took out his watch and looked at it. "They should be on their way home now."

I started to speak but then recalled it was Tuesday. His wife and daughter were returning from their sewing circle, which met in the basement of the First Congregational Church. "Then I shall take my leave. Good day, Mr. Brandt, and thank you."

"It's good to have you home, Priscilla," he said as he sank into his chair and resumed work.

The Brandt's footman answered the doorbell and gaped at me for several moments before recovering his usual stoic appearance. "Welcome back, Miss Llewellyn." He opened the door wider to allow me entry.

"Thank you, Cedric. It is good to be back under this roof."

He shut the door. "Miss Brandt is expecting you. This way."

I followed him down the familiar hallway. "Are they preparing to go in to dinner?" I asked.

"Yes, ma'am." He opened a door and stood next to it. "Miss Priscilla Llewellyn," he announced.

I noticed a slight upturn at the corners of his mouth.

All conversation ceased, and seven pairs of eyes turned towards me.

Grace Brandt was the first to come to me with arms outstretched. "Priscilla, it is wonderful to have you home again."

She embraced me and turned towards the other women. "Priscilla has been away for two years. We're so pleased to have her home."

Melissa was less restrained and threw her arms around my neck. "Nothing has been the same since you left. Please don't go away again."

I kissed her cheek and realized we were both weeping. "We shall talk about that later. It is so good to be with you again."

My friend released her hold on me and stepped back.

I searched the room for Rachel Downs but did not see her.

"I assume you're looking for Rachel," Melissa said. "She had another engagement that would not permit her to come for dinner today. She told me she plans to pay a call on you tomorrow."

I was disappointed but accepted her absence.

"Did you know she married Fred Butler two months after you went to Texas?" Melissa asked.

"No, I did not. Where are they living?"

"They took the house the Butlers lived in before they moved across the street."

"I do not know where that is," I admitted.

"I have the address upstairs. I'll get it for you after dinner."

Other women greeted me before we went to the dining room for the mid-day meal.

Grace, Melissa, and I were settled in the morning room after the other sewing circle members had returned to their homes.

"All right, tell us everything," Melissa demanded. "You so seldom wrote, and when you did, there was no retelling of your adventures. Only that you were someplace and well. There wasn't even an address." She picked up my left hand and rubbed the ring finger. "Why is there no ring on this finger? Where is Mr. Pennyman?"

"There was no marriage, and Josiah Pennyman is most likely burning in Hell."

They looked questioningly at me.

"He died a violent death," I replied quietly.

Their expressions changed to surprise and concern, and they remained silent.

Finally, Melissa said, "What happened?"

I was uncertain how much to tell them. "He was an evil man with dishonorable intentions."

"Oh, my," Grace gasped. "I've heard talk about what transpired in Texas. They're true, aren't they?"

"It depends upon what you heard and from whom," I said, interested in knowing who in Norwich knew about the events in Corpus Christi. "There were times I feared for my life. But I also met some wonderful people."

"A widow was here about a year ago, looking for you," Grace related. "She told peculiar stories about you and a woman named Mrs. Owens, I think." Grace looked at me with a furrowed brow and pursed lips. "I didn't take kindly to her. She told horrendous tales of the goings on at a farm called Gehenna."

"Mrs. Young," I murmured. *But how did she know to look for me in Norwich?*

"Yes, I believe that was her name," Grace acknowledged.

"I met her in Corpus Christi. She was the most unpleasant woman I have ever known, but one ought not to speak ill of the dead," I replied.

"I'm sorry to learn of her passing," Melissa said.

'She was killed last December," I confirmed. I paused to collect my thoughts. "Several people have died. It is difficult to speak of those things."

"I understand," Grace placed her hand atop mine. "Mrs. Young was not a discrete person. She came here, certain you would return to Norwich at your earliest opportunity, and was insistent Mrs. Owens was a murderess."

"Yes, that sounds like Eugenia Young. Elizabeth killed a man while defending me," I said quietly. "I left Norwich in 1866, vowing never to return. There were reminders of Ethan wherever I looked, and everyone seemed to know Papa had betrothed me to Josiah Pennyman. I never mentioned any of you to anyone. It was one of the reasons I did not write. I thought I was protecting all of you. Now, I learn Mrs. Young was in Norwich when I thought I had managed to keep you all a secret."

Grace and Melissa looked from me to each other and back.

"I am sorry, I said through tears. "I never wanted you to know any of this. I have spent the last six months working to put the entire sordid story behind me.

"I live in a Philadelphia boardinghouse and teach French at a girls' school. I have friends there, and I'm happy most of the time."

"Oh, Priscilla," Grace whispered, clutching me to her breast. "We never meant to cause you pain. We've been worried about you. We yearned for letters filled with news of a wonderful new life."

I pulled away from her. "There was no 'wonderful life for me until December of 1866. Elizabeth thought she had a wonderful life with her new husband, but it has become a nightmare."

"Is there anything we can do to help her?" Melissa asked, her cheeks wet and her voice shaky.

"Elizabeth is in Pennsylvania Hospital for the Insane in Philadelphia."

"That's terrible. How did she come to be there?" Grace asked

"Her husband had her adjudged insane because she took steps to prevent him from stealing her money."

"I've heard of men doing that," Grace admitted.

"What can be done about it?" Melissa asked.

"There is a lawyer in Philadelphia working on her release. There may be a hearing or a trial or something...I am uncertain." I said, wiping my eyes with my handkerchief. "I'm so sorry for laying my problems at your doorstep. That was not the intent of my visit."

"Priscilla Cecilia Lewellyn," Grace said sternly. "We are as much family to you as your father and Marian Morrison. My heart breaks to hear all the trouble you've had. You're home now with people who love you. All these things will work themselves out."

"Thank you. I love you all so much. I did not realize how much I missed everyone until I stepped off the train yesterday afternoon." I said, composing myself.

"I heard you have been spending time with Bartholomew Martin," Melissa teased.

"He works for Mr. Osborne. Bartholomew came to Philadelphia to have documents signed. I suppose you know I inherited Aunt Marian's house."

"And a great deal more," Grace added.

I bowed my head. "Yes."

The mantel clock chimed four.

"Is that the hour? Oh, my, I ought to get back to Aunt..."

"Darling girl, you don't have to rush home. Would you like to dine with us tonight?"

"I would love that. I should send a message that I won't be home, though."

"I suspect your servants already know that," Grace said. "Many of them have known you since you were an infant. They'll know you're here."

"I suppose."

"Melissa, take Priscilla upstairs to wash her face and get herself together before your father comes home. Philip and Amanda are coming for supper, too."

"Who's Amanda?" I asked.

"Philip married Amanda Summerfield," Melissa explained, pulling me to my feet and grasping my left wrist. "I remembered her from school but didn't know Philip knew her. Funny thing, he calls her Toby, but neither will say why."

I smiled. "Perhaps we can convince them to tell that story."

Chapter 37

13 June 1868
Norwich, Connecticut

I met with Mr. Forsythe on the tenth and agreed to his suggestions for my investments.

I spent the remainder of the week at home, speaking to the staff and growing accustomed to being the lady of the manor.

Mrs. Ingram, the housekeeper, familiarized me with the household accounts, and we discussed the maids, Mrs. Reese, and the assistant cook. I then had a good conversation with Wilson, who apprised me of the inventory in the wine cellar.

I was forced to admit I knew nothing about wine. He promised to teach me as the need arose. We also discussed the footman, gardener, and coachman.

I asked who to talk with about the cow and chickens. He suggested I start with the gardener and coachman.

My talk with Mrs. Reese was the most fun. We planned the menus for the week. While talking about food stores, we found ourselves in the larder, tasting various dishes cooked the week before I arrived.

At the conclusion of all these discussions, I felt confident about my staff.

Bartholomew visited every evening, sometimes dining with me. We talked much later into the evening than was decent. Neither of us were concerned.

Chapter 38

14 June 1868

I was eating breakfast in the dining room when Wilson announced Bartholomew was waiting in the library.

I wonder why he's here on a Sunday morning. I finished my meal and went to the library. "Good morning, Bartholomew," I said.

"Good morning. Were you planning to attend church services this morning?"

"The thought has occurred to me, but I did not want to go alone, and I had not made arrangements to sit with anyone."

"Come with me. We will sit in my family's pew."

I agreed without a second thought. "I must change my dress." I rushed from the room and up the stairs.

Norris was straightening my room. "What is it?"

"Mr. Martin is escorting me to church."

We quickly changed my dress and pulled out the appropriate accessories.

I returned to the library while Norris went to inform Kloth I had need of the carriage.

We were soon on our way to the First Congregational Church. Bartholomew and I slipped into the Martin family pew from the outside aisle as the organist played the first cords of the processional hymn.

Mr. and Mrs. Martin nodded and smiled. Joseph and Mark,

Bartholomew's brothers, raised their eyebrows and covered their mouths with their hands. They were smacked on the back of their heads by Mrs. Martin, who scowled at them.

An hour and a half later, the service was concluded, and the parishioners filed out by row—the Martins pew was near the center.

"We greeted the Reverend Doctor Hiram P. Arms. The minister grasped my hands. "Priscilla Llewellyn, as I live and breathe. Welcome home, my dear. Are you here for a visit or home for good?"

"I am as surprised as you, Reverend. I am visiting."

"Ah, yes. Marian. My condolences. I know you were close."

"Thank you. I do miss her. I am sorry I was not here when she passed."

"Peace be with you," He made the sign of the cross in the air and looked over my head to the people behind me.

We found Bartholomew's family and greeted them properly.

"It is good to see you again. I pray you had a safe journey," Mrs. Martin said.

I looked at Bartholomew. "We did. Your son went to Philadelphia to escort me to Norwich."

"Did he now," Mr. Martin remarked, taking an interest in our conversation.

"He did. We are enjoying becoming reacquainted." I smiled at Bartholomew. "If you will excuse me, there are a few people I'd like to speak with."

"Of course. Feel free to come to Riverbend whenever you wish," Mrs. Martin offered.

"Thank you," I said and moved towards Rachel and Melissa.

Chapter 39

17 June 1868

After being in Nowich for a week and a half, I had established a daily routine. I spent my mornings handling household affairs, reading and responding to correspondence, and writing lesson plans for the upcoming school year.

Between three and six o'clock in the afternoon, I visited my friends and acquaintances, leaving my calling cards when the ladies were unavailable to me and making it known I would be at home on Thursday afternoons.

Peanut was a frequent companion when I was in the library. She wasn't as playful as she was when she was younger. She enjoyed curling up on my lap or in a puddle of sunshine on the floor.

Chapter 40

20 June 1868

I was in the library, selecting a book to read, when Wilson announced Bartholomew was calling on me.

"Show him in," I said, pulling a volume of Cicero from a shelf and leafing through it.

"Good morning, Priscilla," Bartholomew said. "And, how are you faring this fine day?"

I shut the book and put it back in its place. "The same as I've been since we came here." I turned from the shelf. "How are you faring?"

"Fit as a fiddle.."

"To what do I owe this visit?"

"I have an important question for you.

"You are being cryptic." As I settled into my chair, he lowered himself into the chair across from me.

He stared at me without speaking.

"Bartholomew Martin at a loss for words?" I quipped. "You know nearly everything about me. What do you want to know?"

He cleared his throat. "I...um...that is...may I court you?"

It was my turn to stare. "Mr. Brandt is like a father to me. Perhaps you ought to speak with him before I answer."

He rose and stepped towards me, kneeling at my feet. "I spoke with him yesterday afternoon. He has given his consent."

I reached out to take his hands. "Are you certain?" I asked. My heart was racing.

"I have never been more certain of anything. I love you,

Priscilla."

Words caught in my throat. Ethan Brandt was the only other man to utter those words to me. I took a deep breath and leaned forward. "Yes, and I believe I love you."

He kissed me gently. "I know you must return to Philadelphia. Perhaps I should have waited to ask."

"I am glad you asked. I now have a reason, other than this house, to return. I have obligations there. Not only to the school. I cannot abandon Elizabeth in her hour of need. I will return to stay when I am able."

We stood and embraced.

"Are you not concerned I may be cursed?" I asked.

"What are you talking about?"

"Twice I have been betrothed, and twice the man in question has died."

A laugh escaped him. "No, I am not concerned you may be cursed. Ethan and Pennyman died very differently. You were not responsible for either death."

"Are you going to tell your parents?" I asked.

"They already know I'm head over heels for you. But, I've not told them I planned to ask permission to court you."

"It is Saturday. Shouldn't you be at the office? Are you able to stay for dinner and supper?"

"I worked late yesterday and early this morning. I don't have to go back until Monday. I thought to take you to the sweet shop. They're serving ice cream."

"That sounds nice. Shall we spoil our dinner or go afterward?"

"Afterword. I do enjoy Mrs. Reese's cooking."

"I must admit I have no idea what she is serving for dinner or supper. We discussed menus on Monday, but I cannot recall everything we selected. I do know that she always cooks extra. In the meantime, I was selecting a book to read when you came in. What are you reading?"

He looked away, appearing to be uncomfortable. "Nothing," he confessed. "I don't remember the last time I read for pleasure. Perhaps when the regiment was in winter quarters during the war."

"Well, my darling man, you should also select a book. There is a wide variety here." I swept the room with my right arm. "Choose one or two."

We abandoned the chairs, and I stepped to the shelves where I left off browsing. "Cicero is a little deep for me, though he is completely readable. I am looking for something less thought-provoking, like Mr. Olaphant's novels."

Bartholomew groaned as he looked at books on the opposite wall. "Don't tell me you read that tripe."

"All right, I won't." I moved down the row. "Ah, here's some volumes by Mr. Charles Dickens."

"Not Cicero, but better than Mrs. Olaphant," he quipped as he perused a volume written by James Fenimore Cooper. "Has this library been cataloged?" he asked.

"I have no idea. We ought to ask Wilson or Mrs. Ingram. I have several books upstairs that should be down here." I turned slowly to take in the four walls of books. "I wonder whether all of these books have been read."

"Most of them are in excellent condition. Perhaps they've been read once or twice, but not often."

"And then, there are books like this one." I held the book in one hand and the cover in the other. "A very well-read book." I sat it on the writing table to have it repaired.

We selected books and settled on the settee to read.

"Sitting and reading isn't the most romantic thing a newly courting couple could be doing," Bartholomew observed.

"I disagree. What could be more romantic than sitting with the person you love and reading?"

Bartholomew shook his head. He wrapped his arms around me and kissed me. "Now that is romantic."

"Yes, it is."

At dinner, Bartholomew posed another question. "When do you want to go to Riverbend?"

The query startled me. I had considered visiting the Martins and knew I would have to go eventually, especially now Bartholomew and I were courting. "I shall go when your mother invites me. I shall not intrude on their privacy."

"I'm certain she will extend the invitation soon."

"It will be odd to be there as a guest," I observed.

"Yes, it is. My younger brothers and I continued living at the old homestead after our parents moved to Riverbend. I've been back twice since I moved to the city. It's awkward being a guest in a home you can navigate in your sleep."

After dinner, we walked to the sweet shop and ate ice cream.

Chapter 41

21 June 1868
First Congregational Church
Norwich, Connecticut

The lovely maroon carriage pulled up to the church. Bartholomew stepped down, turned, and assisted me to disembark. He offered his arm, which I took as we approached the sanctuary. Seeing Melissa and Rachel together, I steered Bartholomew in their direction.

"Good morning," I greeted and stepped forward to touch cheeks with each of them.

"I'm so sorry I missed you when you called on me last Wednesday," Rachel lamented. "I was out making calls."

"I was sorry to miss you, too," I replied.

"Bartholomew Martin?" Melissa questioned.

"He works for Mr. Osborne," I stated.

"I know. I also know he wasn't in the office yesterday," Melissa taunted. "Was he, perchance, with you?"

I tried to look innocent and failed. "Perhaps."

"I heard he has called on you every day since you arrived in Norwich," Rachel announced.

"He wants to be certain I am settling in well." I raised my eyebrows. "Is there no privacy in this city?"

"Not between the three of us," Rachel pointed out. "Is he courting you?"

I was saved from responding by a handsome man about

Bartholomew's age coming to stand extremely close to Melissa.

"Good morning," He said into her hat.

"Hello." She smiled. "Mr. Quintin Ross, may I present the elusive Miss Priscilla Llewellyn?"

He bowed and tipped his hat to me. 'I was fearful you were a figment of Missy's imagination."

"How do you do, Mr. Ross," I greeted.

"Shall we go inside?" Quintin asked.

I turned to speak with Bartholomew but found he had gone to greet Fred Butler, Rachel's husband. "I'm waiting for Mr. Martin."

"Which one?" Quintin asked, looking around.

"Bartholomew."

"You're that Priscilla?" he asked, sounding incredulous.

"I suppose I am."

"He never stops talking about you."

I could feel my face grow warm. "He has never mentioned you," I related.

"No reason for him to say anything about me."

Fred Butler and Bartholomew strode towards us.

"Ah, here he comes," Quintin obswerved. "Missy, let's go find your family."

"We'll see you after services," Melissa called over her shoulder as they moved to meet her parents.

Bartholomew touched my elbow. "My parents are in the narthex, waiting for us. Mother is delighted."

Fred and Rachel entered the sanctuary while Bartholomew and I approached Mr. and Mrs. Martin.

Mrs. Martin held out her hands to take mine. "We're so pleased."

"Thank you, I replied. "It is so good to see you again, Mrs. Martin."

"Let's go in. We'll talk after the service."

Mr. and Mrs. Martin led us into the sanctuary and held back

while Bartholomew and I entered the pew. Mr. Martin sat with the center aisle on his left and Mrs. Martin on his right.

After the church service, Mrs. Martin and I waited with other women while carriages, buggies, and wagons were brought to the mounting block.

"Where are you staying?" Mrs. Martin asked.

"Marian Morrison was my godmother. She left her house to me," I explained.

"Oh, goodness, why didn't I know that?" she bemoaned.

"I am surprised Bartholomew hasn't said anything about it.."

"He must have had a good reason." Catherine looked down the line of conveyances. "They tell me men don't gossip. But I know that is not true. There's more gossip passed in the fields and taverns than at any sewing circle."

I laughed. "I did not know that of men."

"You don't have brothers," she pointed out.

"Nor did I spend much time with boys above the age of seven."

"Was that when Bartholomew and his brothers taught you to climb trees?' She smiled and shook her head.

"Yes. We spoke of that incident not long ago."

"Sam and I are delighted Bartholomew is courting you."

"Thank you. I must admit I was taken aback when he asked me. I have always been fond of him, but I never thought of him as a suitor—until he brought the probate documents to me in Philadelphia."

Mr. Martin stopped the buggy alongside the mounting block.

"I'll consult our calendar and send an invitation to dinner at Riverbend," Catherine squeezed my hand, then leaned over and kissed my cheek. "You know you are always welcome there."

"Thank you, Mrs. Martin. I shall look forward to dinner." I walked with her to the side of the buggy. "Enjoy the ride home. River Road is always lovely this time of year."

Bartholomew came to stand beside me. "Goodbye, Mother and Dad. We'll see you at the picnic next Saturday."

We stepped back as Mr. Martin drove away.

"We are being invited to Sunday dinner," I informed him.

"I'm glad," he said. "Oh, here's Kloth with the carriage."

Bartholomew helped me into the conveyance, settled himself, and Kloth drove us to what I was beginning to consider home.

Chapter 42

23 June 1868
First Congregational Church

In the early days of the late war, Mrs. Brandt taught Melissa, Rachel, and me to knit socks for the soldiers and insisted we join the Soldier Aid Society, which met in the basement of First Congregational Church. After the war, the ladies resumed calling the group a sewing circle and provided for their families. I decided to rejoin the group. I gathered my sewing basket and lady's companion and had Kloth drive me to the meeting.

"Priscilla, what a marvelous surprise," Melissa exclaimed when I entered the basement.

"We're happy to have you with us," Grace said. "Will you join us for dinner afterward?"

"I would be delighted. Thank you."

I spent a moment looking around the room.

Two women were using the sewing machines the group had purchased before the war. Others sat in small groups, knitting, crocheting, and hand sewing. Others utilized the long tables and were cutting out the pattern pieces for the garments they would construct.

Rachel, Melissa, and I sat in a corner of the room. As in the past, we were the youngest in the group.

"Where are Hannah and Mrs. Butler?" I asked. I recalled the Bulter ladies joining the Soldier Aid Society when we made the quilt to auction as a fundraiser for the Sanitary Commission.

"Mother Butler and Hannah don't come every week," Rachel reported.

"Is Hanna married?" I asked.

"Sadly, no. She was being courted. I never knew who he was, but he broke it off. Hannah refuses to talk about it," Rachel said.

"I'm sorry to learn that," I said and changed the subject. "I don't see your mother here today. Is she well?"

"She's in good health. Mother had another engagement. She will come to the sewing circle next week."

"Tell me about Quintin Ross," I demanded. "Where did you meet?"

"He's handsome and witty and a perfect gentleman. Fred Butler introduced us."

"What type of work does he do?" I asked.

Melissa puffed up with pride. "He's a doctor."

"Will he be at the Independence Day celebration?" Rachel asked.

"He should be," Melissa said slowly. "He might have to tend to patients."

"Perhaps you should talk to Mrs. Jamison about being a doctor's wife," I suggested.

Melissa frowned. "You're both jealous."

"Why would I be jealous?" Rachel asked. "Fred is home every night at seven o'clock and stays home after supper."

"It appears Bartholomew works regular hours. He sometimes has to go out again if someone Mr. Osborne represents is arrested, but that has only happened twice since I have been in Norwich."

"It isn't so bad," Melissa said defensively. "I rather like having some time without him."

"How long have you been courting?" I asked.

"Three months and four days," Melissa recited.

"Goodness, that is precise," I observed.

"How long have you and Bartholomew been courting?" Melissa smirked.

"We are not courting. We are good friends." I took a few stitches on the handkerchief I was hemming and sent up a prayer asking forgiveness for the lie.

"Ladies, it's time to end our sewing session," Mrs. Brandt announced. "Everyone is invited to my home for dinner."

"I'd love to, Grace, but I'm going to have dinner with my grandchildren," a woman I didn't know explained.

"Family is always first," Grace stated, a slight frown on her face.

I sent my carriage home and rode with Rachel in the cart her father bought her for her eighteenth birthday. *Mayhap I ought to purchase one.*

I returned home around three o'clock and went upstairs after putting my sewing things in a room I called the family sitting room. As I made my way to my room, I paused in front of the closed door to Aunt Marian's rooms.

The door was cool to my touch, and I considered going inside. Rejecting the notion, I continued down the hall and sat at the dressing table in my room to remove my hat. I stared at my reflection in the looking glass. "I miss you so much, Aunt Marian. I wish you were here to share my happiness with Bartholomew and my fears for Elizabeth." I set the hat on the table. *You are being a ninny.*

I stood, marched back to Marian's rooms, took a deep breath, and opened the unlocked door. Her favorite fragrance enveloped me as I stepped over the threshold, leaving the door open. I took a deep breath and felt her presence.

Her sitting room looked precisely as I remembered it. I

could almost see her reclining on the chaise with a book on her lap, a teacup in one hand, and the saucer in the other.

I sank into the chair I typically occupied and took in the room: the curtains, paintings, furniture, and her knickknacks. It was all so familiar yet also strange.

Without conscious thought, I began talking to her. "When I learned Ethan Brandt had died on that battlefield in South Carolina, I thought I would never love again. I left Norwich with a hole in my heart and immense anger with Papa for forcing me to travel far from the only home I had ever known to marry that man.

"I must say, the voyage to Corpus Christi, Texas, was far more enjoyable than I imagined. Save for one man, the crew members with whom I interacted treated me kindly. The ship's captain, Ian McClain, was attentive. We frequently dined together and strolled on deck several times.

"Josiah Pennyman was quite charming when I met him. He lulled me into believing a marriage was possible. As soon as he learned Papa had gone to Africa, he became angry, and my time in Corpus Christi quickly turned into a nightmare. I thank the Lord you shall never encounter that man or the men he employed in Heaven. They are most assuredly suffering the consequences of their evil deeds.

"Aunt Marian, did you know James Kilpatrick is practicing law in Corpus Christi? I renewed my acquaintance with him while I was there. I do not know how Papa knew James was there, but he sent legal papers for me to sign. I learned of this after James helped me leave Josiah's home and a future of abuse and servitude. I was saddened that James and his friends paid a price for coming to my aid.

Oh, Aunt Marian, it was a frightful night. Josiah's men nearly burned the farm owned by a very lovely German immigrant couple while attempting to take me back to Josiah's ranch. Thankfully, we all survived the terror that rained on us that terrible night.

"One of the few good things that happened in Texas was I met Elizabeth Owens. She was employed as a housemaid in Josiah's home. We became friends and traveled from Corpus Christi to Pennsylvania together. We had to change trains many times. There was a man we saw at several stops and came to the conclusion we were being followed. Instead of going directly to her family's home, we detoured to Philadelphia and New York, then back to Gettysburg.

"The man was relentless, Aunt Marian. He hired a Pinkerton agent to follow us. We were so frightened but knew we had to remain stoic. After we arrived in Gettysburg, Elizabeth met a man who began courting her.

"Did you ever travel to Pennsylvania? It is quite lovely, but I never felt comfortable in Gettysburg. I wanted to leave but had no idea where to go until I received a telegram informing me Captain Ian McClain was gravely ill.

"I had grown quite fond of him while I sailed on his ship to Texas. His illness was the excuse I needed to pack my bags and go to him in Baltimore.

"He did recover but was very weak. The doctor did not want him to return to sea immediately, and he had no desire to remain in Baltimore. When he learned I did not wish to return to Gettysburg and seemingly had nowhere else to go, he invited me to observe Thanksgiving with his mother and sister in Ipswich. I accepted.

"You would have liked Mrs. McClain, Aunt Marian. She is a kind and generous woman.

"The man and his sister found me in Ipswich and threatened me. I stood firm that I would not acquiesce to their demands. Augustus Templeton drew a pistol and shot me. I would have died had Ian and the Pinkerton man not acted to pull me backward and push the gun aside. I thought I was frightened when he was following Elizabeth and me, but I was even more scared when that pistol was pointed at me. The man is now in prison. His sister died a most unfortunate death. May she rest in peace." I rose and stepped to the fireplace. "It has been such a relief to not continually look over my shoulder." I fingered the vase on the mantle.

"I thought to become gainfully employed to occupy my time and be productive. I secured a position teaching French at an all-girls school in Philadelphia. The girls are bright and eager to learn. I never knew teaching would be so rewarding."

I moved to the window and stared into the back garden. The flowers were in full bloom, and the gazebo in the center of a small maze looked quite inviting.

"After you died, Bartholomew Martin came to Philadelphia to see me. He is an attorney and works with Nathaniel Osborne. But you probably already knew that.

"Do you remember him? He's the second son of Samuel and Catherine Martin. Their farm is adjacent to Riverbend. You told me many times how you admired Mrs. Martin.

"Bartholomew has visited me quite often. I enjoy his company and have come to realize I have feelings for him. He asked to court me last Saturday.

I wonder whether we will eventually be married. I thought to remain in Philadelphia and teach. After all, I am twenty-four years old and have not met many eligible men living at a boardinghouse full of women and working in an all-girl school. I have been betrothed twice—and both men are deceased. Am I cursed? I pray I am not."

"I find myself thinking about Bartholomew at the oddest times, and I am so comfortable with him. Is that love? I certainly hope so."

I turned and walked into her bedroom. It was a room I had never entered, and I did not recognize anything in it.

The room was sparsely furnished. The bed was narrow. A lamp sat on a small bedside table. A dressing table was the only other piece of furniture occupying the rather spacious room. A wardrobe and chest of drawers were adjacent to one another in the compact dressing room.

All her underpinnings and linen were folded neatly in their places. I felt I was intruding on Aunt Marian's privacy and returned to the sitting room. I tentatively sat on the edge of the chaise but quickly rose and returned to the chair.

It was comforting to tell Aunt Marian about the past two years, though I omitted most of the details. "I will come back to talk again soon," I promised, leaving as quietly as I entered.

Chapter 43

24 June 1868

Intent on purchasing three dresses, I walked to the dressmaker's shop after breakfast.

Odette Imbert was surprised to see me after a two-year absence but went right to work confirming my measurements and showing me fabrics, trims, and images of the latest fashions. She promised each dress would have pockets and a matching reticule.

I left Mrs. Imbert's shop earlier than anticipated and went to the carriage maker's to enquire about a buggy.

Mr. Quigley informed me he had two used buggies in excellent condition and agreed to show them to me. They were similar to the one Papa had given to me. One was slightly smaller than the other, and the roof extended over the footwell. I bought it and arranged to have it delivered to my home that afternoon.

I informed Kloth to expect the buggy and asked whether there was a horse in my stable that was suitable for pulling it. He assured me there was.

I left Kloth and went upstairs to change dresses before Rachel and Melissa arrived for dinner.

The three of us sat in the library, chatting and giggling like schoolgirls.

"How is married life, Rachel?" I asked.

"It's wonderful." She smiled and started to speak but then closed her mouth.

"What aren't you telling us?" Melissa demanded.

"Nothing," Rachel said defensively. "I have nothing to hide. Not a thing."

"You want to tell us something," I said, looking at her more closely.

Rachel clamped her lips together and refused to speak.

"That means only one thing to me," Melissa declared.

"And what would that be?" I asked.

Rachel raised her eyebrows but remained mute.

"She's with child," Melissa announced.

"How did you know?" Rachel protested.

"You're positively glowing," Melissa explained. You've been married for nearly three years. A baby is the only thing that would make you glow like this."

"is it true?" I asked.

Rachel nodded.

"When?" Melissa asked.

"Dr. Jamison says January or February."

"Oh, how exciting," I exclaimed.

"What about you, Priscilla?" Rachel asked.

"I am most definitely not with child," I asserted.

"Is Bartholomew Martin courting you?" Melissa asked.

"We are friends, nothing more," I lied.

"If you say so," Rachel looked skeptical. "You make a handsome couple, and you've been seen sitting in the Martin family pew at church."

"I have not paid the subscription to restore the Llewellyn pew. Besides, I dislike sitting alone."

"If you insist. It certainly looks like he's courting you."

"Don't be silly. He knows I am returning to Philadelphia."

"It looks like you're establishing yourself here. I saw Mr.Quimby helping Kloth move a very handsome buggy into your carriage house. I noticed some of the furniture in this house has been rearranged, and ornaments are missing from tables on the mantles and tables in the library and drawing room."

"I have made some minor changes. Some chairs needed reupholstery, and a few ornaments I never cared for have been put in storage."

"What about the buggy?"

"I want to be able to drive myself on occasion. I do not want to use the large carriage all the time."

Melissa and Rachel exchanged a glance.

"All right, I understand what you're saying. But, you wouldn't be doing all this if you didn't intend to return to Norwich."

Wilson saved me from commenting further by announcing dinner was ready to be served.

Chapter 44

4 July 1868

During the past two weeks, messages were exchanged between households to coordinate the Independence Day picnic preparations.

Mrs. Reese spent the week cooking and baking while Mrs. Ingram and Wilson coordinated packing the wagon with furniture, table linen, dinnerware, and food.

I felt guilty about not having anything to do save selecting the dress I would wear that day.

I enjoyed a leisurely breakfast and lounged in the library reading until ten o'clock.

I went upstairs to change and found Norris already in my room, with my dress laid out on the bed and the jewelry atop the dressing table.

I went down to the kitchen to find my staff rushing to and fro.

"Good morning, Miss Llewellyn," Mrs. Ingram acknowledged. "The wagon is almost packed, and the staff is nearly ready to leave for the park."

"That's wonderful," I replied, watching the apparent chaos. "Mr. Martin and I shall be leaving for the park at half past twelve. I believe we are dining at one. Is that correct?"

"Yes, ma'am. I haven't heard from any of the housekeepers

this morning, which I take as a good sign."

"Happy Independence Day," I called to the staff and returned upstairs.

Bartholomew and I arrived at the park on time and easily found his parents and two younger brothers.

Mrs. Reese and Catherine Martin were busy checking the various dishes before sending Yancy and a young man I did not recognize to put them on the table.

"Who is that with my footman?" I asked.

"Oh, that's Kenneth Underwood. He's one of Mother's orphans. He's considering going into service," Bartholomew informed me.

"He will not have a better teacher than Yancy and Wilson," I observed. "I am considering hosting a party before I return to Philadelphia. I will talk with Wilson about retaining Kenneth as an extra footman."

"I'm certain Kenneth would appreciate the practical experience."

When the other families arrived, more food was placed on tables that were already threatening to collapse under the bounty.

I looked around as we were preparing to sit down. "It appears most of the city is here."

"We've always been a patriotic city. It's even more so with so many veterans of the recent war. Have you ever seen so many ill-fitting blue sack coats?"

I smiled. "What regiment were you in?"

He straightened his perfectly tailored sack coat and smiled. "I was a regimental clerk for the Sixth Connecticut

Volunteer Infantry; I saw my fair share of fighting but spent most of my time mired in paperwork."

After the mid-day meal, the older men wandered to the beer garden while the ladies brought out their needlework and chatted.

Melissa, Rachel, and I gravitated towards each other, with our gentlemen following. Several other people we had known at school joined us as we began to settle near the baseball diamond.

"We must move from here," I overheard Melissa say to Bartholomew.

"Why? There's a game about to start, and we have a lovely spot under these trees," Bartholomew asked.

Rachel picked up on the conversation and agreed with Melissa.

"I repeat, why?" Bartholomew asked, still confused by their adamant conviction.

Philip rolled his eyes. "Ethan first caught Priscilla's eye while he was playing baseball at this picnic in 1860. I introduced them while the grand march was being formed. Melissa is being overprotective. Priscilla hasn't been to an Independence Day picnic in Norwich since that summer."

"Stop it!" I shouted.

Everyone stopped what they were doing and stared at me, horror written on their faces.

"I can hear what you are saying. I am well aware of what happened in this park eight years ago. I was there. It happened to me. Ethan taught me the rules of baseball. We talked about the game and frequently watched it being played.

"Yes, I was formally introduced to Ethan at the dance that night. I've been to balls since then and haven't collapsed with grief.

"I am here today with Bartholomew Martin, a wonderful man who has become quite dear to me and who has many fine qualities. I am looking forward to dancing with him tonight. And, no, I will not be thinking of Ethan Brandt any more or any less than I normally do. Ethan will always live in my heart. So will Bartholomew."

No one moved. No one spoke. Even the baseball players had stopped to listen to me.

Bartholomew spoke first. "I never doubted your feelings for me." He moved closer to me. "I'm looking forward to dancing with you tonight."

"Thank you," I whispered. "May we stay right here, under these trees? Please?"

"All right, everyone. The lady wants to stay right here, near the baseball game," he shouted.

The baseball players cheered and began the game.

"Toby, let's sit here with Priscilla and Bartholomew," Philip said, spreading a blanket on the ground.

"Why do you call her that?" I asked.

"I have my reasons," Philip quipped.

"Do you mind being called 'Toby'?"

"It's an endearment," Amanda Summerfield Brandt told me.

"I suspect there is a story behind that endearment. Perhaps someday you will favor me with that tale," I turned my attention to the baseball field, where a batter was already at every base.

After supper, we wandered to the outdoor theatre for a lyceum and enjoyed poetry readings, a string quartet, and singing and dancing.

Finally, there was dancing at the base of the bandstand, where a small orchestra sat. As tradition dictated, the mayor and his wife led the grand march, which ended in two lines, ready for a reel. We danced through the fireworks.

Chapter 45

12 July 1868
Riverbend Farm

The day I had been dreading since agreeing to return to Norwich had arrived. I dressed carefully and paced the downstairs rooms, waiting for Bartholomew to escort me to church. I looked out a window and saw that Kloth had already brought the carriage around.

I hadn't heard the knock on the door and was startled when Wilson announced Bartholomew's arrival.

"Good morning," he greeted as he crossed the room to stand before me. "You look especially lovely today."

"Thank you. I want to make a good impression on your parents."

"There's no reason to be nervous. They've known you since you were an infant and already love you."

"I am not so nervous about being with them as I am about returning to Riverbend. Has it changed very much?"

"I don't know. I never spent much time inside the manor house. The farmland has changed only slightly. The horses and sheep are still there. More land is planted in crops."

"I would like to go to the mausoleum today, if I may. I want to talk with my mother."

"I can't imagine my folks having any objection to that. We will walk there after dinner."

A clock chimed.

I picked up my reticule and gloves from a nearby table. "We

should be leaving. We do not want to be late for services."

Following the church service, we greeted Reverand Arms and spoke with a few friends and acquaintances before boarding the carriage for the trip to Riverbend Farm.

We spoke very little during the seven-mile ride. My anxiety increased with every mile. I sat a bit straighter when we passed the turn to go up the drive to Calamus, the farm owned by Amos Downs, Rachel's father. "We are halfway there," I uttered.

"I have always used Calamus and Riverbend to gauge the distance to Martin Farm, as well," he told me. "Oh, look, that old crooked oak tree fell. I wonder when that happened."

"I was always fearful it would fall across the road when I traveled to Norwich," I related. "I know it was a silly notion."

"Not at all. I had the same fear for years. It started leaning before the war. I think I first noticed it about ten years ago. It finally leaned a bit too far."

"It is sad. I wonder how old it was. But, look, there are saplings around where it stood. In a few years, there will be several large trees in place of the one," I indicated to the space where the tree had stood.

"And we'll have the pleasure of watching them grow."

The carriage made a sweeping turn to the right, throwing us to that side of the carriage.

"We are near the manor house," I said, grasping his hand and looking out the window for a glimpse of my former home.

Kloth turned right and then left to halt the carriage in front of the steps to the house my grandfather built—the only home I had known until my father sent me away.

I expected the house to look different, but it was the same as I remembered it. I half-expected Duncan to open the door when we climbed the steps to the porch, but he did not.

"I thought I heard horses out here," Mark said when he

opened the door.

"Priscilla, this is my brother, Mark. Do you remember Priscilla?"

"Hello," he said, opening the door wider so we could enter. "I do remember you. Bartholomew and I taught you to climb trees."

A giggle escaped me. "Is that the only memory you two have of me? I recall more interaction than tree climbing."

"It's the only time I got a whipping for teaching someone to climb a tree," Mark explained. "It stuck with me."

"Who's at the door?" a male voice asked from behind Mark.

Mark looked over his shoulder. "Tell Mama that Bartholomew and Priscilla are here."

"I don't know where she is. Papa is in the family parlor." the voice said.

"Oh, sorry," Mark said. "Priscilla, this is Joseph, our younger brother. Joe, have you ever met Priscilla Llewellyn? She used to live in this house."

Joseph came up behind his brothers. "Hello. Sorry, I don't remember you, but I'm always being reminded that I'm the baby of the family. A lot happened before I was born."

"Nice to meet you, Joseph. I do recall you as a baby."

"Why don't we go into the family sitting room?" Bartholomew suggested, taking my shawl and hanging it on the hall tree. "Joe, Mother is probably downstairs in the kitchen. Will you go down and let her know Priscilla is here?"

"Sure." He turned on his heel and trotted towards the staircase to the service level.

Bartholomew touched my elbow and guided me towards the family parlor.

It had always been one of my favorite rooms. The lighting was superb for sewing and reading and was a good size for a family to gather in the evening.

Mr. Martin was sitting in Papa's chair, reading a newspaper, but looked up as we entered the room. "Good afternoon, Priscilla. It's good to see you again."

"You just saw her an hour ago," Mark smirked.

"Watch your mouth, son," Mr. Martain instructed.

"Yes, sir."

"Please sit wherever you're comfortable," Mr. Martin invited.

I hesitated before sitting with Bartholomew on the settee. I allowed my gaze to wander around the room. It was exactly as I remembered it, including the paintings on the walls. "Are you comfortable here?"

"Yes, we're very comfortable," Mrs. Martin answered. "How are you, my dear?"

"I am well. It is surprising you left my family portraits. I expected them to be stored in the attic or sold."

"Oh, Priscilla, we didn't have the heart to remove them. They are the history of this home, Catherine Martin explained.

"We suppose your father took the portrait of you with him."

"Father never commissioned it done," I explained, a tinge of regret in my voice.

"We shall have to rectify that," Mr. Martin declared.

"Perhaps someday," I said vaguely.

Joe, Mark, please help me put dinner on the table," Mrs. Martin directed. "The girls are having their dinner at the Swensons."

The two young men jumped to their feet and followed their mother to the kitchen.

I thought it odd the family had no house staff, but said nothing.

"We should go to the dining room. Mr. Martin set aside his paper and led the way.

The table was set for six with three places on each side. Mr. and Mrs. Martin occupied the center chairs—across from one another. Bartholomew and I were seated on either side of his mother, with his brothers across from us.

Mr. Martin said grace, and the dishes were passed around as they were at Mrs. Peele's. We were all hungry and ate without conversation for several minutes.

"Your roast is delicious, Mrs. Martin," I extolled.

"Do you enjoy cooking?" she asked.

"I am afraid I cannot boil water. Mrs. Farnsworth cooked for Papa and me for more than twenty years. I have been living in other people's homes since I left Norwich. And, now, Mrs. Reese is cooking for me at Aunt Marian's house."

"How do you manage in Philadelphia?" Jacob asked.

"I live in a boardinghouse. Mrs. Peele and her daughters cook for us."

"It's nice you have money to employ people to care for you," Mr. Martin observed.

I smiled. "Tell that to my lady's maid. I was not permitted one when I went to Texas and had to learn to dress myself. Norris is frustrated that I frequently dress without her assistance."

"I've never had the luxury of a lady's maid. I wouldn't know what to do if I had one," Mrs. Martin declared.

"I would let Norris go, but she tends to my clothing, something I can do, except for the laundry," I added. "I am aware I have lived a privileged life, very different from the way Bartholomew grew up. I did not know a day's work until I began teaching last year."

"What do you teach?" Mark asked.

"I teach French at a girls' school. It's a combination high and normal school. If the girls stay through graduation, they are qualified teachers. Sadly, many drop out when they are sixteen to work, care for siblings, or marry.

"Please, tell me about Riverbend. What crops have you planted this year?"

Mr. Martin warmed to the subject. "We're growing wheat, alfalfa, and root vegetables at Riverbend. I've continued the tradition of using seeds from the previous crop to produce the following season.

"At Martin Farm, we're experimenting with the grains and have expanded the vegetables to sell in Norwich."

When we arrived, I saw the horses and sheep. Are you still breeding both?"

"Yes. In fact, we had several foals born last spring. Joseph, here, has been learning to train horses and shows great promise."

"Is Fenwick instructing you?" I enquired.

"Yes," Joseph confirmed. "He's remarkable."

"I would like to see him again, if I may," I stated.

"You should go out to the horse barn after dinner. He moved into the barn after your father sailed to Africa," Mr. Martin shared.

"I expect you'd like to visit the mausoleum, as well," Mrs. Martin said.

"Yes, I planned to go out there," I murmured.

I helped clear the table after everyone had eaten their fill. Mr. Martin assured me the boys would wash up, and Bartholomew and I should walk about the farm.

We struck out for the Llewellyn Mausoleum, built by my great-grandparents shortly after the war for independence from England. Though the day had warmed, the air in the shade of the ancient trees was cool.

The mausoleum was a large stone building with three generations of Llewellyns within its walls. I grew up expecting to lay my father to rest in that building. It saddened me to know he will now repose in eternity someplace in Africa.

The wooden door had recently been sanded and refinished to a beautiful dark walnut color. Bartholomew opened it and indicated that I should enter. He followed.

Despite the early summer afternoon sun shining through the stained glass window high on the southern wall, the air was fresh and the temperature comfortable.

The coffins bearing John and Priscilla Llewellyn, my great-grandparents, rested on pedestals in the center of the main room. Six of their nine children lay in tiny coffins in a row against the western wall.

On the northern wall were my great uncles, Michael and Simon. They had lived to adulthood but died in separate farming accidents before either married.

My grandparents, John II and Constance Llewellyn, were laid to rest along the eastern wall. Seven small niches in the wall above their caskets held the remains of their seven babies who never drew a breath.

In a room to the left, or north, another room housed a solitary casket in which my mother, Cecilia Redburn Llewellyn, reposed.

Before entering the north room, I introduced Bartholomew to my relatives in the main room. Bartholomew paid his respects to my mother, then discretely left me alone with her.

I placed a bouquet of wildflowers we picked in the meadow atop her casket and said a prayer before greeting her. I stood with my right hand resting on the lid of the plain wooden box. I started speaking slowly as I explained why Papa had not been to see her, then launched into my story, beginning with leaving Riverbend in April 1866 and ending with the moment I entered the stone building.

During the one-sided conversation, I laughed and cried and lamented the loss of her and my father. I finally ran out of things to say. Looking through the doorway, I saw the light patterns on the floor had changed.

"I must go, Mama. I promise to come again before I return to Philadelphia." I leaned over and kissed the coffin, then straightened, wiped the tears with my fingertips, and left in search of Bartholomew.

We walked through the meadow, enjoying the early summer day. We came to the corner of the horse barn and stood to watch several mares grazing and their foals frolicking in the knee-high grass.

We entered the horse barn and stood momentarily, allowing our eyes to adjust to the comparative darkness. Then, we walked through the barn, glancing into the empty stalls.

"Who's here?" a familiar voice demanded.

"Is it all right to pet the horses?" I called, a smile spreading to my eyes as Fenwick came down the center aisle.

"As I live and breathe," he uttered, quickening his step. "Miss Priscilla. I never expected to lay eyes on you again."

"I never expected to be back here, either. You are looking well," I replied. "Do you remember Bartholomew Martin?"

"Sure, how you doing, Mr. Bartholomew?"

"Just fine," Bartholomew replied.

"Buck is still with us," Fenwick reported.

"What about Gwen?" I asked.

"She's out in the pasture with her twins."

"When did you decide to breed her?"

"We didn't. She did it all on her own."

"There must be a story there."

"No story. She somehow got into the pasture with the stallions. They did what horses do."

"Is she a good mama?"

"Appears to be. Her foals are close to weening. It'll be a couple of years before we can train 'em, though."

"I do recall Papa complaining of the uselessness of the foals until they were two or three and could be ridden."

"We have a good breeding schedule, so we have a nice supply of rideable mounts."

"You are looking well, Fenwick."

"I'm real sorry to hear about Mrs. Morrison." He cocked his head towards the dooryard. Them two horses you have hitched to your carriage are beauties."

"They should be. They came from this farm," I quipped. "Kloth takes great care of my livestock."

"Your livestock?" Fenwick's eyebrows were raised.

"You knew about Aunt Marian passing. How is it you did not know she named me her heir?" I asked.

"I ain't been to town since..." he stopped speaking and closed his eyes while tilting back his head. "My goodness, it must be nigh on four or five months since I been to town."

Bartholomew touched my elbow. "Pricilla."

I understood the hint. "I suspect I'll be back to Riverbend sooner than later. Bartholomew and I are courting."

A smile sprang from his mouth to his eyes. "Your papa would be pleased with this match. He worried about you something fierce after Mr. Ethan passed." He turned his attention to Bartholomew. "You take good care of our girl. The farm hands are partial to Miss Priscilla."

Bartholomew grinned. "I'll keep that in mind. There's a couple of them I wouldn't want to cross."

The smile left Fenwick's face. "You don't want to cross any of us, boyo. She's as much our little girl as she is her Papa's daughter."

"Yes, sir. I'll keep that in mind." Bartholomew glanced around the barn. "We ought to go. It's getting late."

"Goodbye, Fenwick. I'll be back soon." I said.

Bartholomew and I turned and returned to the manor house to say goodbye to his family.

Chapter 46

13 July 1868

I sat at the breakfast table, sorting the morning mail, when I came across a letter with Beulah's name on the return address. Unceremoniously ripping open the envelope, I unfolded the pages and commenced reading.

Dearest Priscilla,

All is well at the boardinghouse. Mrs. Peele, Miss Crane, and Calah send their best wishes.

Mr. Green visited me this evening. He has engaged a doctor to examine Jeanne. We are quite hopeful this doctor will be able to certify her as sane.

Daphne Crane has been attending Sunday services with me, and we keep each other company after supper. Miss Adams accuses me of turning Daphne against her. She can't see that she's done it to herself. It's very sad.

I saved sufficient funds to purchase my own horse and buggy. Neither is much to look at, but I am able to travel to and from the asylum in much less time than when I rode the street cars.

We're all anticipating your return.

Best Regards,
Beulah Snodgrass

I set the letter on the table beside the unused spoon and leaned back in the chair. "This is good. This is very good." I sighed, pushed back from the table, collected my mail, and went to the library to pen a reply.

Chapter 47

15 July 1868

I was growing anxious to know whether the doctor Mr. Green engaged had been afforded the opportunity to examine Elizabeth. I determined to write to him after supper. As it was, there was no need for me to set pen to paper. A letter from Mr. Green was waiting for me when I returned home from making social calls.

Dear Miss Llewellyn:

I retained Dr. Emma Zuckerburg, a gynecologist with a superb reputation. She examined Mrs. Finch at the asylum on the eleventh of July. I received the doctor's written report on the fourteenth.

Dr. Zuckerburg found Mrs. Finch to be of sound mind.

I have petitioned the court for a hearing and am now awaiting a date from the court. I will write again upon receipt of that notification.

Best Regards,
Paul Green
Attorney at Law

A smile spread as I read the letter. Elizabeth was one step closer to being a free woman.

As I sat at the table in the library after supper, writing letters to Agatha and Beulah, it occurred to me that Elizabeth should not immediately return to Gettysburg. It was a distinct possibility Oliver might attempt to harm her or attempt to have her sent to another asylum. *Dare he try?*

I included this concern in my letters. *Where ought we secrete her?* I determined to discuss the matter with Bartholomew.

After writing the letters, I sat on the settee with my unshod feet tucked under me and tried to read. Thoughts of Elizabeth in that horrible asylum repeatedly broke my concentration. Peanut sensed my restlessness. She jumped onto my lap and circled around before jumping back onto the floor and settling herself in a chair to sleep.

I closed the book, unfolded myself, and went upstairs to bed.

Chapter 48

20 July 1868

It seemed the ink was barely dry on the last letter from Mr. Green when another arrived.

> *Dear Miss Llewellyn:*
>
> *The court has set Mrs. Finch's hearing for 14 September 1868 at 10 AM.*
>
> *It would be helpful if you testified at the hearing. You met Mr. Finch and conversed with him before his marriage to Mrs. Finch. Since the school term will have begun before that date, I will have a subpoena issued for you to testify.*
>
> *Please make an appointment to meet with me upon your return to Philadelphia.*
>
> *Best Regards,*
> *Paul Green*
> *Attorney at Law*

Testify? To what? I was contemplating this when Bartholomew entered the library.

"What's troubling you?" he asked, crossing the room and kissing my forehead.

Without speaking, I held out Mr. Green's letter.

Bartholomew took and read it, then looked at me. "Are you concerned about testifying?"

"Yes. I have never been in a courtroom. How do I dress? How do I comport myself? What do I say?"

"You wear a nice day dress. You answer the questions posed to you as honestly, succinctly, and politely as you can, using a voice loud enough for the entire room to hear you. Mr. Green wants to meet with you, probably to discuss what information he will seek."

"What can I tell him that I haven't already said?" I asked, taking back the letter and laying it on the table.

"Likely nothing, but the court needs to hear it from you because you witnessed behaviors others haven't." He grasped my hands, pulled me from the chair, and wrapped his arms around me. "Don't worry about it. You'll be fine."

I looked up at him. "What could I possibly have to say? I am not a doctor."

"No, you're not, but you've met Oliver Finch and had conversations with him. You've seen him and Elizabeth together. And you knew Elizabeth before she met Oliver Finch."

"I attended the supper party where they met," I said quietly.

He released his hold on me, and we moved together to the settee.

"What has that to do with whether she's sane?" I wound my arm around his and leaned my head on his shoulder.

"The judge needs to know about their relationship prior to the marriage and how she managed her affairs. Was she dependent upon someone to manage them for her, or was she able to manage them herself?"

"We each managed our affairs." I had a second thought about what I said. "Well, James Kilpatrick was helping to settle the issues surrounding the business Papa invested in during the war. Apparently...well, you already know about all that."

"Sadly, yes, I do know about it. I'm grateful James was in

Texas, and he was able to come to your assistance."

"I am as well."

We sat quietly, lost in our thoughts and hearing sounds from the open windows.

"Do you have plans for Wednesday next?" Bartholomew asked.

"Nothing out of the ordinary," I replied, curious why he was asking.

"I received an invitation to a reception honoring Governor James E. English at the home of Mayor Lorenzo Blackstone," he announced. "I don't want to go alone, and I thought you would enjoy it."

I stared at him for some moments, disbelief writ on my countenance. When I recovered sufficiently, I replied, "I will inform Kloth we shall need the carriage. How did you come to be invited to such an event?"

"I haven't a clue. The invitation came to the office in the afternoon post."

"I wonder who else will be there," I mused.

"I believe Mr. Osborne also received an invitation." Bartholomew looked at me and squeezed my hand. "Perhaps he knows how I came to receive the invitation.

"It has been years since I attended a reception, and never for someone so august as the governor. I shall look forward to the evening."

He kissed the side of my head. "This will be our first social engagement together."

"That fact makes it even more special." I smiled. "Miss Adams must have known something about us that I did not."

"Who is Miss Adams?" Bartholomew asked.

"The rude woman at the boardinghouse. She is usually quite severe and judgemental. One night after you came to have the probate documents signed, she stated that she suspected I should soon be leaving the boardinghouse to be with you."

He did not immediately respond. "I knew that weekend I wanted to spend the remainder of my life with you."

I leaned away from him, staring. "I felt an attraction but never thought to see you again. I was reticent to think about being courted. I am so pleased you came to escort me to Norwich."

"I confess it didn't happen as I told you. I began planning to court you when Mr. Osborne told me he needed me to go to Philadelphia to sign the documents. I was delighted when he informed me you would be coming to Norwich to finalize the transfer of assets."

The tall clock in the hallway chimed nine.

Bartholomew stood and looked down at me. "I must go home, but I shall see you tomorrow."

"I'll let Mrs. Reese know you will be here for supper." I stood on tiptoes and kissed him.

"Bless you for taking pity on a poor, suffering bachelor who has no one to cook for him."

I rang the bell, and Wilson came.

"Mr. Martin is leaving."

"Yes, ma'am. I shall retrieve his hat."

Bartholomew kissed me again. "I shall see you tomorrow."

Chapter 49

29 July 1868
Home of Mayor & Mrs. Lorenzo Blackstone

Bartholomew and I arrived at the Blackstone residence on Washington Street shortly after eight o'clock. I allowed my gaze to take in the décor in the foyer and hallway as we waited our turn through the reception line. The house was tastefully appointed in hues of green and ecru. I did not recognize any of the people in front of us and wondered who they were.

"Oh, look. Isn't that Bartholomew Marton? Who is that with him?" A masculine voice behind us called out.

I turned to my companion. "Who has recognized you?"

Bartholomew glanced over his shoulder. "No one I would ever introduce to you."

"I thought we knew the same people." I smoothed the front of my dress and tugged on the cuff of my gloves.

"I was acquainted with him when we were in college."

"You were not friends?"

"Most assuredly not. We were in a couple of classes together, and I recall him being in a study group I joined my sophomore year."

The Blackstone's butler announced us as we moved towards Mayor Lorenzo Blackstone and his wife, Emily.

Bartholomew bowed over Mrs. Blackstone's hand and shook the mayor's.

I nodded to the first couple of Norwich.

"Are you Michael Llewellyn's daughter?" Mayor Blackstone

asked.

"Yes, I am," I replied.

"He is a fine horse breeder and trainer. Our stable master thinks quite highly of him and his skills."

Curiosity animated my features. "Did you know my father?"

"Did he pass?"

"Not to my knowledge. He took passage to Liberia on a ship owned by the American Colonization Society."

"How very peculiar." The mayor pursed his lips and appeared to be in thought.

Mrs. Blackstone extended her hand, which I took. "It is lovely to make your acquaintance, Miss Llewellyn."

"Thank you for inviting us," Bartholomew said.

The mayor turned to the Governor. "May I present Miss Priscilla Llewellyn?"

"Llewellyn..." Governor James E. English murmured. "We met many years ago. You were quite young. I was at Riverbend to meet with your father before the war."

"It is an honor to meet you, sir," I said, slightly dipping my head. "It is kind of you to remember my father."

"Yes, yes. Enjoy the evening, Miss Llewellyn."

I nodded my response and turned towards Bartholomew. "It seems everyone in this state knew my father."

"His breeding and training skills are renowned. Your father and Fenwick are the best horse trainers around. Enjoy the notoriety."

I pushed out my lower lip. "I suppose all that notoriety goes to your father and Fenwick now."

"Yet, everyone remembers your father, not mine."

The conversation lapsed as we stood near the entrance to the ballroom and gazed at the guests.

Bartholomew tilted back his head and smiled before guiding me across the room to join a group of people about our ages.

As Bartholomew began to make introductions, the man

from the reception line burst into the group. "Ah, there you are, Martin. What have you been up to? Found employment yet? Or are you still working on Daddy's farm?"

"Simon Granger, why don't you go talk with someone else?" one of the other men suggested.

Simon ignored the comment and turned to me. "Why are you associating with a ne'er-do-well like Bartholomew Martin?" He reached out to touch my arm.

I stepped backward three steps. "Please do not touch me," I said softly.

"Think you're too good for the likes of me?" Simon sneered.

"We don't want any trouble. Why don't you go outside and get yourself under control?" another of the gentlemen suggested. "You're embarrassing yourself and the young woman."

"I'm not embarrassed." He again directed his speech to me. "Are you?"

"As a matter of fact, yes, I am."

Bartholomew touched my elbow. "Let's go, Priscilla."

"We're just getting acquainted," Simon said, stepping towards me.

"The lady doesn't want to know you, Simon," Bartholomew said. "Go away."

I saw one of the other men raise his hand as though signaling for someone serving champagne.

A footman came. The man whispered to him. He looked at Simon, then searched the room and left, now holding an empty tray.

"I haven't seen you since we graduated, Simon. How are you keeping yourself busy?" asked a man I thought I had met previously.

He pulled himself to his full height. "I am a gentleman farmer.

"In other words, you are unemployed," Bartholomew said.

"I oversee my family estate," Simon boasted.

"You're calling that broken-down farm an estate?" someone sneered. "Have you ever known a day's labor?

Simon glared at the man. "Jasper Hightower, I'll have you know improvements have been made. We expect a bountiful crop this autumn." He puffed with pride but was once more rebuffed.

"Will you harvest a bushel of corn?" Jasper asked.

"Enough," Bartholomew exclaimed. "We are here to honor the governor, not insult one another." He turned to Simon. "I hope you have great success with your family farm. Now, I believe it is time for you to say good night before there is a brawl."

"Thank you," Simon responded, returning his attention to Bartholomew and me. "But I have no intention of leaving so soon. Aren't you going to introduce me to this lovely lady?"

"No," Bartholomew spat. "You made improper advances on the lady. You have not earned an introduction. I suggest you learn to be a gentleman in the true sense of the word."

Simon pushed Bartholomew in the chest with his index finger. "Who asked you to tell me what to do and how to behave? You're a flunky in what used to be a one-person law firm."

"I shall make no effort to disabuse you of your opinion of me. And I shall protect the lady I am escorting tonight from the likes of you." He looked over Simon's shoulder to his college friends. "Gents, we'll get together another time." He saluted them, touched my elbow, and guided me towards another corner of the room.

We did not speak of Simon Granger for the remainder of the evening.

Chapter 50

30 July 1868

My time in Norwich was drawing to an end. Mrs. Ingram reminded me there were decisions to be made regarding the disposition of Aunt Marian's personal effects.

With the exception of storing away some knick-knacks and rearranging some of the furniture, the house remained as it was the day my godmother died.

I had repeatedly returned to Aunt Marian's rooms to speak with her. During the last visit, I realized her essence was in every room of that house. I need not pace her private sitting room to speak with her. The morbidness of keeping her rooms intact and closed was not lost on me, either. I called Mrs. Ingram and Norris to the library to announce we three would go upstairs and decide the fate of Aunt Marian's most personal possessions.

Many tears were shed over the course of the day, but the decisions were made. Norris and a housemaid would pack her clothing and shoes to be donated to the poor farm.

One can never have too many handkerchieves, and I kept all of hers. Some Aunt Marian had embroidered herself.

As executor of Aunt Marian's estate, Mr. Osborne had taken her jewelry to Tiffany and Company in New York City for appraisal. Upon his return, the most valuable pieces were placed in the safe in his office. I made an appointment to look at the pieces.

Three necklaces, two tiaras, and four rings were in Mr. Osborne's safe. All were exquisite pieces. I decided to keep all of them for myself.

I spoke with Mr. Osborne about selling some of the pieces at the house that I did not care for. He promised the sales would be discreet.

When I returned home, I sat in the library, an open book in my lap and my thoughts elsewhere. I suddenly remembered I had furniture in storage in New Orleans that ought to be brought to this house.

I immediately went to the writing table and wrote a letter to Jacob Smythe, the purser on the merchant ship Emma, asking that he take my possessions out of storage in New Orleans and arrange for delivery to my home in Norwich.

I paused as I wrote the words "my home," realizing it was likely the first time I referred to the house as my home rather than Aunt Marian's house. It made me smile.

Peanut jumped up on the table and tried to walk across the letter. I picked her up and looked into her face. "You cannot be walking across my letters, young lady," I scolded, then held her close to my chest and buried my face in her furry neck before setting her on the floor.

Melissa came into the room as I was finishing the letter. "My, you seem to be in a good mood."

"I am," I replied, telling her all we had done during the week.

"Am I to understand you will be returning to Norwich permanently?" she asked, waving her left hand about wildly.

"I believe it does," I said, attempting to capture that elusive left hand. "Bartholomew and I are courting. I think he wants to propose marriage."

"Well, then I beat you to it," Melissa gloated, once again moving her left hand about.

I finally captured it and looked at the stunning opal ring on her finger. A new piece of jewelry?" I admired. "When did Quintin give it to you?"

"Last night. He finally gathered the courage to ask Papa's permission."

I hugged my friend. "I am so happy for you. Have you set the date?"

"Not yet. We'll likely do that before the party my parents are hosting to announce our betrothal. All the parents are pleased with the match."

"That always makes things easier." I tugged on the bell pull and waited for Wilson to come. "We'd like tea and cake, Wilson."

"Yes, ma'am," Wilson backed out of the room.

"Let us sit," I said, moving from the table to the settee. I suspect Bartholomew will talk with your father again before the end of the year."

Melissa smiled but said nothing.

"I know that expression," I accused. "What do you know that I do not?"

"Who? Me?" she feigned innocence. "Why not a thing." She batted her eyes.

"I will allow you to keep your secret—for now."

Wilson brought the tea.

The afternoon was filled with idle gossip and tea.

Part 3
Elizabeth and Priscilla

Chapter 51

21 August 1868
Norwich, Connecticut to Philadelphia, Pennsylvania

Batholomew insisted on escorting me to Philadelphia.

Melissa and Rachel met us at the railroad depot to see us off.

Rachel and I hugged. "I'm going to miss you," she said through tears.

"You will be too busy preparing for the baby." I released her and turned to Melissa. "And you will be so busy planning your wedding, you won't have a spare moment to think of me." We embraced.

"You're returning to your life in Philadelphia and won't give us a second thought, either." Melissa retorted.

"I will be back in Norwich for Christmas," I pledged and looked at Bartholomew. "I promise to write regularly to all three of you."

"Just don't write in French," Rachel quipped. "I doubt I could conjugate a single verb—if I could remember the verbs."

"I shall dutifully correspond in English." I crossed my heart with a gloved index finger.

The conductor shouted, "All aboard."

Bartholomew touched my arm. "Priscilla, we must go."

"Goodbye. I'll see you in December," I called as he led me towards the nearest passenger car.

We found seats and settled ourselves for the brief trip to New Haven.

There was a three-hour delay between arriving in New York and leaving for Philadelphia. Bartholomew and I decided to leave the station for an early supper.

We found a restaurant not far from the station and ate a lovely meal in near silence.

"I'm going to hate not being able to see you every day," Bartholomew said as we returned to the train station.

"You are going to miss Mrs Reese's cooking," I teased, hugging his arm. "I will be lonely without you. But you will be busy with your clients. Don't you have a trial starting in a few weeks?"

"How do you know that?"

"The day after I arrived in Norwich, I had an appointment with Mr. Osborne. You came in from court and told your clerk to put the trial on the calendar, It must have stuck in my head."

"Holy cow."

We walked another block before we spoke again.

"Do I recall correctly that Elizabeth's hearing is also in September?" he asked.

"Yes. I'm meeting with Mr. Green next week. I will go to see Elizabeth tomorrow."

"I wish I could go with you, but I'll be on the first train back to Norwich."

"I know. You really didn't have to escort me, but I am very happy you did." I hugged his arm.

We arrived in Philadelphia and took a cab to Mrs. Peele's boardinghouse. The boarders were still at supper when Bartholomew and the cab driver took my trunk upstairs.
The cabbie returned to his carriage while Bartholomew and I said our goodbyes in the foyer.

"I will write," I vowed again.

"I will, too," he said. "I'll also stop by your house to assure myself the servants—ah, staff, as is you prefer—are faring well."

"You just want Mrs. Reese to feed you," I teased.

"You're on to me," he rejoined, then grew serious. "I will be counting the days till you come home."

"You must not keep the cab waiting," I said, opening the door. "December will be here before we know it."

He kissed me again and gently rubbed his thumb across my cheek. "Good night," he whispered, walking briskly to the waiting cab.

I walked into the dining room, where everyone was enjoying dessert. A slice of cake and a cup of tea were at my place. I sat. "Hello, everyone. I trust you are all well," I greeted as I slipped onto the chair and placed a napkin on my lap.

"I see you are thick with that young man," Miss Adams observed.

"Your prediction of my association with Mr. Martin proved correct, Miss Adams. Mr. Martin and I have been courting since July."

Beulah squealed and clapped her hands.

"I suspected as much," Miss Adams replied in her stiff manner.

Agatha nodded with a napkin to her mouth.

"What other news do you bring with you?" Miss Crane enquired, her eyebrows raised.

"I had a lovely time with my friends. I will be returning to Connecticut for Christmas." I picked up the fork, cut off a piece of the cake, and put it in my mouth.

"Did you sell your godmother's house?" Beulah asked.

"No. I decided to keep it and its staff."

"Did you go to your family's farm?" Agatha asked.

"Yes, twice." I set the fork on the plate. "Bartholomew and I were invited to a Sunday dinner with his family. The second time, I went by myself to the Llewellyn Mausoleum. I did not bother anyone at the manor house. I wanted to spend time with my family."

"How very touching," Miss Adams sneered. "Especially since you didn't know any of them in this life."

"Miss Adams, why are you so venomous? I have never done any harm to you, yet you repeatedly verbally attack me." I began to shake with anger.

"Well, I never..." Miss Adams began.

"You have been mean to Miss Llewellyn since the day she moved here," Miss Craned interrupted. "I have never understood why until I received a letter last week."

"Who would be writing to you?" Miss Adams spat.

"Your sister," Miss Crane replied calmly. "I learned you know far more about Miss Llewellyn than you ever let on."

"You know as much as I do," Miss Adams replied.

"Why did you never tell me you were related to the Templetons?"

I felt the color drain from my face as I stared at Miss Adams.

"Would you please repeat that?" Agatha asked.

"Miss Adams and the Templetons are cousins." Miss Crane elaborated.

Miss Adams glared at me and pointed a finger across the table. "You are responsible for the deaths of Eugenia and Percival and for Augustus rotting in some prison in Massachusetts."

I stared at her. "Percival Templeton was attempting to kidnap me when he was shot dead. I have been told Eugenia wanted to surrender to the police but was being dragged onto a train by Augustus when she was shot in the back by a bullet meant for her brother. Were you aware Augustus Templeton attempted to extort money from me and then tried to kill me?"

"Eugenia..." Miss Adams began, then stopped speaking. She

pushed back her chair and fled the room. Her footfalls echoed on the stairs.

An uncomfortable silence enveloped the dining room as we finished eating the cake.

"Excuse me," I said. "I will go up and unpack." I took the stairs slowly, thinking about the dismal homecoming. *This is no longer my home.*

Chapter 52

25 August 1868

Agatha and I left the rooming house at two o'clock and hailed a cap to carry us to Mr. Green's office.

"Good afternoon, ladies," Paul Green greeted. "I trust your time away from Philadelphia was enjoyable, Miss Llewellyn."

"It was. Thank you," I returned. "Miss Bentley and I visited with Mrs. Finch on Saturday. She is hopeful for a future outside the walls of that hospital."

"I'm pleased her spirits are high," he replied.

"I have a grave concern about Mrs. Finch's case," I said. "Do you know the judge's opinion of women physicians?"

"I'm given to understand he has no such proclivities," Mr. Green confided.

"Perhaps you ought to engage a male physician sympathetic towards women in these situations. Surely, there are one or two in this city."

"I assure you there is no need to go to that length," Mr. Green said confidently.

I skeptically glared at the attorney.

"Dr. Zuckerburg has impeccable credentials. The judge will certainly accept her diagnosis." He looked at a paper on his desk. "Tell me about Mr. Finch. You're the only person in Philadelphia, aside from Mrs. Finch, who has met him."

"Elizabeth and I met Oliver Finch at a dinner party at her sister's home. She found him fascinating and allowed him to call on her. Something about him unsettled me. He seemed

213

controlling, though he did nothing outwardly to give me that impression. I declined most invitations to join them when they were going to lectures and concerts.

"Elizabeth rarely talked about him with me. I overheard conversations as I passed the sitting room or entered the room unexpectedly. He sometimes sounded overbearing, as though he was scolding a child.

"I thought she was a little too free with showing him valuable items she owned. For instance, he purports to be a jeweler and owns a shop in Gettysburg. Elizabeth has five gold nuggets taken from her first husband's gold mine in California. She gave them to him to assay and appraise. These five nuggets' total weight is nearly one pound."

"Do you know where the gold is now?" Mr. Green asked.

"No, I don't. We would have to ask Elizabeth where she kept them after she married Oliver," I replied.

"I suspect she has them secreted away somewhere. She took precautions to protect her money and other valuables, including her house. I would think anything that could be carried away in a pocket would be placed someplace private for safekeeping," Agatha offered.

"I gave you the letter I received from the lawyer who is trustee of her trusts. Perhaps you can contact him about the location of the gold," I suggested.

"It's of little import at the moment. We must concentrate on this upcoming hearing." Mr. Green paused as he consulted his notes. "

"Will anything I say at the hearing be of any help to Elizabeth?" I asked.

"I think your testimony will be helpful. You met Oliver Finch and observed how he behaved with Mrs. Finch."

On the way back to the rooming house, I admitted to Agatha that I wasn't as hopeful for a good outcome for Elizabeth as I had been before this meeting.

Chapter 53

14 September 1868
Philadelphia Courthouse

I was nervous entering the newly built courthouse behind Independence Hall, but I found a seat in the gallery and waited for Elizabeth's case to be called.

It was jarring to hear the clerk read her name and to see Irene Davidson escort her to sit beside Mr. Green. Mrs. Davidson took a seat beside me.

Mr. Green called me to testify. After promising to tell the truth, I stood in the witness box and answered all his questions in a clear voice.

Mrs. Davidson testified about Elizabeth's exemplary behavior while a patient at Pennsylvania Hospital for the Insane in Philadelphia. She repeatedly referred to Elizabeth as Jeanne Zigler, explaining that Oliver had her admitted to the hospital using that name. Employees were forbidden from addressing her as Elizabeth Finch.

Mr. Green called Elizabeth to testify, but the judge did not allow it. Therefore, his next witness was Dr. Emma Zuckerburg. She had a kindly face and spoke with confidence. After reciting her credentials, Mr. Green asked whether she had examined Elizabeth. "Yes, I spoke with her at great length. I found Mrs. Finch to be quite charming. She is bright and articulate. She is oriented to time and place. She is quite capable of caring for herself. Mrs. Finch understands why her husband had her judged insane. It is my professional opinion that she does not suffer from female hysteria or any other mental defect and is able to reenter society."

After the doctor stepped down, the judge leaned forward to address Mr. Green. "Do you have any other medical opinions related to this case?"

"No, your honor," Mr. Green replied.

"Is Mr. Finch in court?" the judge asked.

There was no response.

"In that case, I find Mrs. Finch remains insensible and is confined to Pennsylvania Hospital for the Insane in Philadelphia." He dropped his gavel on the desk and said, "Next case."

We were stunned at the decision. How could he come to that conclusion?

"Had I known which judge was hearing this case, I would have recommended you have him recused," Dr. Zuckerburg stated. "His decision has nothing to do with the merits of the case or whether I am a woman. His wife was recently diagnosed with female hysteria and was admitted to the Pennsylvania Hospital for the Insane."

"I am willing to testify on Mrs. Finch's behalf again, but I believe you ought to contact this man." She held out a slip of paper to Mr. Green. "Dr. Asher does not subscribe to all this falderal about women's propensities. Having the opinion of a male doctor in these cases will always be favorable to the court."

Mr. Green looked at the paper in his hand. "Thank you. I will talk with him this afternoon."

"How soon will we be able to file a new petition?" I asked.

"We should wait several months before trying again," Mr. Green advised. "I'm afraid she'll be spending yet another

Christmas in that place."

I left the courthouse, discouraged and angry with Mr. Green. When I walked into my classroom, I was relieved to see Esme Tremblay Alden instructing my students.

After supper, I returned to my room and wrote to Bartholomew, telling him all that transpired in court.

Agatha and Beulah settled on my bed while I finished writing his address on the envelope and sealing it. I then turned my chair around and gave my friends my full attention.

"So, how are we going to get her out of that place? And when?" Agatha asked.

"I cannot take her to Norwich until Christmas," I said. "That gives us three months to plan her escape."

"We must include Irene Davidson in our scheme," Beulah stated.

"I agree, " I said. "Do you and she ever have the same days off?"

"I've been thinking about that, too," she replied. "I can trade with another cleaner. Give me a week or two to make the arrangements."

Agatha stifled a yawn and looked at my alarm clock. "Is that the time? We're up past our bedtimes. Let's talk more about this tomorrow." She stood and left my room.

"Goodnight, Priscilla," Beulah said as she followed Agatha.

I sat in the chair a long while after my friends sought their pillows but finally fell into bed and slept fitfully.

Chapter 54

26 September 1868

A letter from Bartholomew lay on the foyer table when Agatha and I returned from visiting Elizabeth.

He assured me Mr. Green could engage another doctor and file a new petition. He was confident this was a setback but was not a final result.

Bartholomew also extended greetings from his mother and assured me our friends and his family were looking forward to my return to Norwich in December.

His words, identical to those spoken by Mr. Green, were comforting, and I speculated when the new petition might be filed with the court.

I sighed, set his letter aside, and picked up the book on my bedside table.

Chapter 55

4 October 1868
Fairmount Park
Philadelphia, Pennsylvania

True to her word, Beulah arranged a day off when Irene Davidson was not working at the asylum. Agatha and I met with them at Fairmount Park—the largest park in the city.

We can't wait for Mr. Green to find a doctor the judge will listen to," I started. "I want to take Elizabeth to Norwich."

"When do you want to do this?" Irene asked.

"The Saturday before Christmas," Agatha replied.

"It won't work," Irene stated. "The ladies aren't allowed to walk outside in the snow."

Agatha and I groaned.

"Of course. We didn't think of that," Agatha conceded.

"The snow won't melt until April or May. The spring term ends May 28," I mused.

"Mr. Green may have been successful by then," Beulah observed.

"Let us formulate our plan, just in case he's not successful. Again," I said.

"We visit her on Saturdays," Agatha said aloud, looking at the sky. Would someone suspect us if she disappeared on a Saturday?"

"Perhaps not. Some people would notice if you were not there, but not if you were." Irene replied.

"Wouldn't we be the most likely suspects, though?" Agatha

asked.

"That is also true. You two will most likely be suspected regardless of the day of the week she disappears," Irene pointed out.

"May 30 is a Sunday and Decoration Day," I announced. "Most people will go to church and then to the cemetery to decorate graves and have their family picnic. They are less likely to be visiting someone in any asylum."

"That might be a good day," Irene agreed. "How do you propose to secrete her out?"

"Priscilla and I have been thinking about that," Agatha admitted.

"Are you planning to leave at the same time?" I asked.

"Yes. I'm ready to seek a new position," Irene admitted.

"Let Agatha and me work out how to remove you and Elizabeth most inconspicuously. Do you trust us?" I asked.

"If I didn't trust you, I would not be here," she confided.

"Please don't tell me your plan," Beulah pled. "If I don't know, I can't tell."

That evening, I wrote to Bartholomew, telling him we had devised a plan. *He will likely advise us to abandon the plan,* I thought while addressing the envelope.

Chapter 56

21 November 1868

I lay in my narrow bed, listening to the rain pelting the window and missing Bartholomew. Writing letters was a poor substitute for having him beside me.

A gentle knock brought me out of my reverie. Believing it to be either Agatha or Beulah, I called out, "Come in."

Miss Crane pushed open the door carrying a tea tray. "Happy birthday, dear girl."

I struggled with the heavy blankets covering me to sit up, smiling all the while. "Thank you. How did you know?"

"A little bird told me." Her smile reached her eyes.

"There are two cups," I observed. "Please sit and share a cup with me."

The older woman poured out, handed a cup to me, and then settled in the chair at the foot of the bed. "We've had no opportunity to talk since you returned," Miss Crane began. "I want you to know I think you are a courageous young woman. Not many people speak to Barbara Adams as you have. Not even me."

"Why did her sister tell you about the Templetons?" I had been curious since I learned of the correspondence.

"I don't know. We are not well acquainted. Barbara's sister has had an easier life than Barbara."

"I regret being so blunt with her." I sipped my tea. "Mmm, Earl Gray. One of my favorites."

"Mine, too," she admitted. "As far as I can tell, Eugenia

Templeton Young did not tell Barbara the whole truth of her activities with her brothers. She was horrified when you told her Augustus tried to kill you."

"Did you know Percival and Augustus were identical twins?" I asked.

Her eyes widened for a moment. "No, I did not."

We sipped our tea, seemingly having exhausted the subject of the Templetons.

Miss Crane finished her tea, set the cup on the tray, and stood. "I'll leave you to dress. Breakfast will be served soon."

"Thank you, I said, holding out my empty cup for her to take. "I will dress and be downstairs for breakfast."

She nodded, picked up the tray, and stopped in the doorway. "I would like it if you called me Daphne. Miss Crane makes me feel old."

"I would like you to use my Christian name as well."

As soon as the door closed, I threw back the covers and swung my feet to the floor.

I was downstairs before seven o'clock. I noticed the drawing room door was closed as I passed through the foyer. *That is odd,* I thought and continued to the dining room.

Miss Adams and Daphne Crane were the only occupants.

"Where is everyone?" I took my place at the table.

"Calah is with her family," Daphne ticked off on her fingers. "Beulah and Agatha have yet to come down."

"Strange. I heard Agatha's door creak while I was dressing," I related. "Thank you, again, for the tea, Daphne. I enjoyed our little talk."

"You took her tea?" Miss Adams glared at her friend.

"Yes, I did. It's her birthday, and I thought a cup of tea in bed might be a nice way to start the day."

"You've never brought me tea on my birthday," Miss Adams

226

spat.

"You once told me you didn't enjoy lounging in bed," Daphne countered. "I shall mark my calendar to bring you tea on your birthday."

Beulah and Agatha came in during the last statement.

"Who had tea in bed?" Beulah asked.

"I did. Miss Crane brought it to me," I confessed.

"I love snuggling under the blankets with a lovely cup of tea." Beulah's voice had a dreamy quality.

"I always thought it too much of a bother," Agatha stated.

Faith and Hope placed breakfast on the table.

"I'll be right back with the tea," Hope announced.

"Thank you," I said, spooning scrambled eggs onto my plate.

"Where is your mother this morning?" Miss Adams asked.

"She had an early morning appointment." Faith offered no further explanation before returning to the kitchen.

As the meal neared its end, Agatha asked. "What are your plans for the day, Priscilla?"

"I had thought to visit Elizabeth, but the rain has changed that plan. I'm giving a test to my fourth years next week. I may begin composing it today."

"I've not been to the Museum of Natural History in some time. Would you like to go with me? Agatha asked.

"Thank you, but no." I patted my face with my napkin and pushed back from the table. "I will be upstairs." I had a foot on the bottom step when someone rang the doorbell.

Sighing, I removed my foot, pivoted, and opened the door.

Bartholomew stood on the stoop, holding an umbrella.

"Oh, my goodness," I gasped and moved aside to allow him entrance.

He closed and shook the umbrella before stepping into the

foyer. "Good morning."

"Why are you here?" I took the sodden umbrella and placed it in the stand.

"It seemed the best way to celebrate your birthday." He kissed me. "Happy birthday."

"Mercy, I have never had so much fuss over my birthday."

"I assumed your father gave lavish parties to honor the day." He smiled and gazed into my face.

"He blames me for Mama's death. Papa usually spent my birthday at the mausoleum."

He glanced towards the dining room. Seeing the other boarders still at the table, he rubbed my upper arms. I'm so sorry. I had no idea."

"Mrs. Farnsworth, our cook, always made a cake. Melissa and Rachel would come over with small gifts. Sometimes, they spent the night."

"Shall we go into the drawing room?"

"No," exclaimed Agatha as she emerged from the dining room. I mean, you can't. Mrs. Peele is in there with someone.'

I raised my eyebrows, questioning her statement. "Faith said she had an appointment."

"The appointment is here. In the drawing room." Agatha fidgeted, obviously flustered.

"Why don't you get your wrap? I have a carriage. We can go out," Bartholomew suggested.

I nodded and dashed up the stairs.

I felt guilty about riding inside the carriage while the driver was being drenched by the rain. "Perhaps we should go someplace where your driver can get out of the rain."

Bartholomew spoke with the driver, then settled back in the seat.

"Where are we going?" I asked.

"The hotel has a respectable public lobby. We can go there and talk."

"I'm happy you are here," I said, glancing at him. "When did you decide to come?"

"I decided the day after you left Norwich. It's not the same without you there." He reached over and caressed my cheek.

"I know. I actually miss my house. Mrs. Peele and her daughters are good cooks, but I miss Mrs. Reeses' meals," I stared out the window. "I love teaching French, but I have begun counting the days until I can return to Norwich."

"I have a calendar in my flat where I mark off the days," he confessed. "Not to change the subject, but I want to talk with you and Agatha about your plan to remove your friend from the asylum."

"Do you think it folly?" I asked. "Mr. Green is interviewing doctors again, but I have no faith that the judge will ever allow her to rejoin society. He seems to dislike women."

"Your plan could work, but it will be dangerous. I don't like the idea of you being hurt."

"I have learned the diagnosis of 'female hysteria.' It is ridiculous. There seems to be no medical basis for it." I informed him.

"I know. I've been reading up on it myself. I spoke with Dr. Jamison. You are correct—there is no medical basis for the diagnosis. If a doctor says the magic words in front of a judge, the poor woman is branded insane. Having the decision reversed is a most difficult procedure. I am sorry your friend is going through this."

"If Mr. Green has not been successful by the end of May, Agatha and I will get her out of that horrid place."

"You understand that I cannot help you," he stated.

"I would not ever consider involving you in this. Could I be charged with kidnapping?"

He considered this question for some moments. "If she

walks off the hospital grounds of her own volition, I would not think so. I do caution you and your friends that she must be alone when she leaves the grounds. You may be on the public street outside the hospital, but do not accompany her until she is on the public street, also."

I took in what he said and thought through our plan. "We can do that."

"Please, don't tell me the details," he implored. "We must keep this conversation theoretical."

I nodded.

Bartholomew and I ate dinner at the hotel restaurant before returning to the boardinghouse.

Upon entering the house, I went upstairs to put my paletot and hat in my room.

He waited for my return at the foot of the stairs. The moment I opened the drawing room door, I realized why it had been closed.

The furniture had been pushed against the walls, leaving the center open and bare. A huge fire burned in the fireplace. Friends I had made in the community and at school came to say goodbye.

A cup of punch was thrust into my hand as I made the rounds, thanking everyone for coming.

Following a buffet supper, a cake was brought from the kitchen. I blew out the lit candles, though I refused to count them. We all ate cake.

Soon, all the guests except Bartholomew were gone, and I stood in the foyer, saying good night.

"I will come in the carriage to take you to church," he announced.

"Agatha, Beulah, and Daphne will be coming, too," I reminded him.

"That's great. I enjoy the company of your friends."

"You will like Daphne. She can be the life of the party."

He smiled, leaned in, and kissed me. "I hope you had a good day."

"I did—in no small part because you are here. I'll see you in the morning."

He left the house, and I shut the door, touching my forehead to it. I prayed, asking Bartholomew to be kept safe from harm.

Mrs. Peele and her daughters were cleaning after the party. I fleetingly thought of helping but decided to go upstairs to my bed.

Chapter 57

22 November 1868

The rain had turned to snow and was beginning to stick.

Bartholomew rang the bell at half past seven.

Beulah, Agatha, and Daphne offered to walk the few blocks to the church, but he insisted they ride with us.

The carriage was spacious but seemed close, with our crinolines smashed together. Bartholomew elected to sit with the driver.

The five of us sat together in a pew nearer the front than the back, with Bartholomew at the center aisle and me beside him. Agatha, Daphne, and Beulah sat slightly apart from us.

Heavenly fragrances filled the house when we returned to the boardinghouse.

"Someone's been baking," Daphne observed.

"There's something else," Beulah sniffed. "There's a spicy odor I can't quite place.

"Perhaps cinnamon?" Agatha suggested.

Bartholomew chuckled. "There's only one way to find out." He stood at the dining room door while we filed in and took our places, then sat beside me.

"When do you return to Norwich?" Daphne asked.

"There is an eleven o'clock train to New York," he replied. "I have a seven o'clock appointment tomorrow morning."

"Goodness," Beulah exclaimed as she passed the plate of pancakes to Daphne. "Do you always start your day so early?"

"Fortunately, no. Sometimes we must accommodate our client's schedules. This particular gentleman has an eight o'clock appointment with the jailer."

"So, you handle criminal cases?" Agatha asked.

"I do, but not exclusively. We have our share of civil matters."

The conversation lapsed as we ate.

I accompanied Bartholomew to the railroad station and watched the train move towards New York before returning to Mrs. Peele's house, consoling myself that I would soon be on that train.

Chapter 58

8 December 1868

Agatha and I had not been to visit Elizabeth since the first snowfall in November, and I missed those weekly visits.

I was considering writing to Irene Davidson when Beulah burst into my room without knocking.

"What is wrong?" I asked, panic in my voice as I looked at her disheveled appearance. "What's happened? Are you all right?"

"I...have...a...message...," she panted, holding an envelope in her outstretched hand.

I took the envelope and set it on the table. "Why are you so out of breath?" Has something happened to Elizabeth?"

She removed a knitted scarf from around her neck and unfastened her paletot. "I ran from the livery stable."

Agatha stood in the doorway. "What's all the commotion? Is Elizabeth all right?"

"No," Beulah said flatly. "She's been injured."

"What's..." I started to ask but picked up the envelope and ripped it open.

> *Mrs. Zigler was rushed to Philadelphia Hospital this afternoon. She is expected to recover, but her injuries were too severe to be treated by our physicians. She will be returned to us upon release from the hospital.*

Meet me at Mrs. Doyle's Tea Shop at four o'clock tomorrow afternoon.

Irene Davidson

I dropped the missive on the table. "What happened?"

"Mr. Ziegler came for a visit. He was angry that she petitioned the court to be set free."

"That hearing was nearly three months ago. Why did he wait so long?" I asked.

"I don't know. I only know he came onto the ward screaming that she shouldn't have filed the petition. Before anyone could reach them, he grabbed her by the hair and began slapping her." Tears ran down Beulah's face.

I handed her a handkerchief.

"Jeanne called for help, but none came. He took something from a pocket in his overcoat and waved it in front of her. I saw it was a knife.

"One of the orderlies rushed over to restrain Mr. Ziegler and got his arm cut for his trouble.

"Mr. Ziegler held the knife to Jeanne's throat and said he ought to kill her right then, but that would give her the easy way out. She needed to suffer for making him look a fool.

"Another orderly managed to take away the knife, but Mr. Ziegler began punching Jeanne and threw her against the wall.

"She twisted around and tried to escape him, but he grabbed her arm and slammed it against the edge of the window. There was a terrible cracking sound, and she cried out in pain.

"Then, he threw her to the floor and began kicking her. "She managed to crawl under a nearby bench, but he drug her out and stomped on her chest and stomach and lower limbs, then resumed kicking her in the head and side.

"Finally, four orderlies were able to get firm grips on his

upper and lower limbs. He shouted and wriggled to get free while they carried him from the ward.

"Jeanne lay on the floor, moaning and holding her arm. Her dress had been torn. She managed to roll to her back. Bruises and cuts covered her face and arms. The nurses said her corset helped protect her body." Beulah stopped talking. She was shaking from head to toe. Tears streamed down her cheeks. Pins had fallen from her hair, which hung around her face and down her back.

Slightly more composed, she continued. "The matron and I moved Jeanne to her room and laid her on the bed.

"Three doctors came and examined her. They determined our hospital didn't have the supplies to treat her and called for an ambulance. They took her to Philadelphia Hospital at Eighth and Pine."

Anger and revulsion consumed me as Beulah finished her abhorrent tale.

"Why does Irene Davidson want to meet with us?" Agatha asked. "We should go to the hospital. They may allow us to see her,"

"We must notify Mr. Green," I said quietly. "He should be aware of this attack."

Agatha looked at the watch pinned to her dress. "It's nearly seven. Mr. Green is likely leaving his office for the day. This outrageous attack must be considered very carefully."

"I'm going to clean up before supper." Beulah wiped her face and pushed her hair back before slowly walking to her room.

"I wonder whether they had him arrested," I murmured.

"I don't think he did anything illegal. Men are allowed to physically abuse their wives. I have little appetite, but let's go down to supper."

Chapter 59

9 December 1868
Mrs. Doyle's Tea Shop

Agatha and I arrived early at the tea shop. We ordered tea and pastries for three and then waited for Irene Davidson.

She arrived while Mrs. Doyle was setting the teapot on the table.

"I am sorry to keep you waiting," she said, removing her cape.

"We came directly from the school, so we were a few minutes early," Agatha explained.

"How is Elizabeth?" I asked.

"I was with her before I came here. She has a broken arm and several cracked or broken ribs. Her face and body are severely bruised. She's suffering from something the doctors call 'brain commotion.' I'm told that means in the course of his attack, he did something that bruised or injured the brain. She's livid he was allowed to beat her without any legal penalty.

"The good news is that Mr. Finch has been expelled from the hospital and is not permitted to see her as long as she's a patient there."

"Gosh, he only had to attempt to kill her to be banned from seeing her." My acerbic tone was not lost on either of my companions.

"Has Mr. Green been informed of Oliver's actions?" I asked.

"I haven't spoken with him," Mrs. Davidson admitted.

"We'll inform him." Agatha poured out the tea.

"Thank you," I said. "How long will she be at the hospital?"

"I don't know. The doctors say she must remain in bed for several weeks. We are not equipped to care for her under those circumstances."

"Would we be allowed to visit her?" I asked.

"I believe so. Mr. Ziegler...Mr. Finch has not prohibited it," Mrs. Davidson admitted.

"Does he know she is at Philadelphia Hospital?" I asked.

"I don't know that, either. I've not seen him since he was expelled from our hospital." Mrs. Davidson cut off a piece of her pastry and sipped her tea.

"We should go after school tomorrow," Agatha suggested.

"Are you going out of town for Christmas?" Mrs. Davidson asked.

"Yes, I'll be in Norwich," I replied.

"I'll spend the holiday with my family in Gettysburg," Agatha explained. "I plan to visit Elizabeth's sister while I'm there."

"Do you have plans for Christmas?" I asked.

Mrs. Davidson shook her head. "I have no family. I always volunteer to work so the women with families can be home. I'm certain you will both have wonderful visits."

"That is very generous of you," I observed and decided to do something for her.

Mrs. Davidson pulled on her cape and gloves. "I have another appointment, but I will keep in touch with you."

"Enjoy your evening," Agatha offered.

We watched her wend around the tables and exit the shop.

"We should be going as well. I have papers to mark," I said, placing several coins on the table and adjusting my cape on my shoulders.

Chapter 60

21 December 1868
Norwich, Connecticut

Kloth met me at the train station and drove directly to my house. I was surprised to see the house had been decorated for Christmas. The fires in library and my bed chamber lent a cheery air to the rooms.

"Has the Christmas tree been ordered?" I asked Mrs. Ingram.

"Yes, ma'am," the housekeeper replied. "It will be delivered tomorrow."

"Good. After I sent messages to you and Wilson, I sent invitations for the tree-decorating party on Wednesday."

"Mrs. Reese has been baking. We shall be ready for the evening. Kloth and Yancy will bring in the tree Wednesday morning," she informed me.

"That's wonderful," I exclaimed. "Mr. Martin will be joining me for supper this evening."

"Yes, ma'am. I believe Mrs. Reese is preparing something special for your supper."

I scowled. "I wish she would not, but there's nothing for it now." I ran a finger down my list. "I believe that's everything for now. I appreciate all of you staying with me."

"I shall relay your gratitude to the staff."

I turned towards the stack of mail on the table. Bartholomew had taken out all the bills and important-looking correspondence, but several that required my immediate attention remained.

"Good evening, Priscilla." Bartholomew broke my concentration as he entered the library and strode towards the table where I had been sitting all afternoon.

"Goodness, what is the time?" I asked, looking up from a letter I had been reading.

"How long have you been sitting there?" he asked, kissing my cheek and looking over my shoulder.

"Most of the afternoon." I set the letter on the table and stood. "I had no idea there would be so much correspondence. I should have these letters sent to me in Philadelphia."

"I should have thought of that," he said. "I'll start sending you the mail I don't handle for you."

"I am capable of handling my financial obligations." I moved around to the settee.

"I thought you arranged for Mr. Osborne to continue managing your affairs."

"He does handle my legal matters. Mr. Forsythe is my financial manager. But, I am perfectly capable of satisfying my debts, even from Philadelphia."

"You should speak with them about making those arrangements if you're serious about doing it yourself."

"Perhaps I shall, but not this week." I heard footfalls outside the door. "I believe supper is being served."

The door opened, and Wilson appeared.

Chapter 61

23 December 1868
Norwich, Connecticut

The Christmas tree was brought inside and placed in the foyer. I was reminded of Christmas in 1864 when Papa became angry about the noise Fenwick and Duncan, our butler, made while bringing the tree into the house. It was during the war, and Papa thought it frivolous to have a decorated tree inside the house when so many men were dying on the battlefields across the country.

Although only four years had passed, it seemed a lifetime since the incident.

I sighed and watched as the tree stood straight and tall in the curve of the staircase.

Mrs. Ingram came to me wringing her hands. Her brow was furrowed, and she gave the distinct impression that something was distressing her.

"What is it, Mrs. Ingram? Surely nothing could be that awful two days before Christmas."

"There's a large package been delivered from Riverbend, ma'am. I was told what it contains but haven't had it opened."

"What have the Martins sent? Surely it's not terrible."

"They sent your family Christmas decorations and tree ornaments, ma'am."

I thought the poor woman would burst into tears. "That was

very thoughtful of them. Have the box sent up, and we'll mix them with Aunt Marian's." I patted her hands. "Don't be so distressed. It's a wonderful thing. Perhaps we ought to have another Christmas tree in the library."

She looked up. Astonishment replaced distress. "Are you serious, ma'am?"

I had commented in jest but thought having a Christmas tree in the library would be nice. "Yes, I believe I am. Instruct Kloth to obtain a smaller tree for the library." I smiled. "New life. A new tradition."

"Yes, ma'am. I'll speak with him. Is there anything else, ma'am?"

"I think not. Continue with preparations for the party."

She nodded and left to go about her duties.

Perhaps we will put trees in other rooms next year. I laughed and went to the library to sort the morning mail.

Melissa arrived early and sat on the divan in my room while I finished dressing.

"Two Christmas trees?" she gasped.

"Two Christmas trees," I confirmed. "It is a logical solution. I planned to have one tree decorated with Aunt Marian's ornaments. But, then, the Martins sent the Llewellyn decorations. I want to use both collections. So, I ordered a second tree for the library. One of the maids and I spent three hours dividing the tree ornaments so half will be on each tree."

"That was a thoughtful gesture," Melissa agreed. "Which one will you place the gifts under?"

"The only gifts under the library tree will be those Bart and I give to one another. All the other gifts will go under the tree in the foyer."

"You may have started something. Quintin and I may have two Christmas trees next year." Melissa smiled.

"You look beautiful. That green is a perfect color for you," I complimented.

"That deep red is stunning. Is it new?"

"Yes. I wrote to Madame Imbert and asked her to make a dress for Christmas. I'm quite fond of it."

The mantel clock chimed, and I looked at it. "Oh, goodness, I need to get downstairs. My guests will be arriving soon."

The tree decorating party was a success. The novelty of having two Christmas trees was the talk of the evening.

I was thrilled to see the ornaments of my childhood hanging side-by-side with those collected by Aunt Marian, which also had special memories for me.

Bartholomew was the last to leave. We sat on the library settee, enjoying the unlit tree. Several ornaments reflected the firelight, giving others a festive glow.

"I am delighted your parents sent my family decorations to me. It was very thoughtful." I smiled.

"It was Mother's idea. She wanted to send them to you the first year you were gone but didn't have an address for you," he related.

"It's just as well. By December of 1866, I was in Ipswich. Very few people knew where I was." I fell into the memories of Captain Ian McClain's childhood home—his mother and sister. It was a gentle reminder to write to Mrs. McClain.

It had been two years since I accompanied Ian McClain to Ipswich for Thanksgiving and stayed until after the new year. *I must write to Mrs. McClain.*

"Hello. Where are you, Priscilla?" Bartholomew asked, lightly tapping my shoulder.

"I'm sorry. I fell into some memories. Mrs. McClain and her

daughter were very kind to me. I brought horror to their doorstep, but they never blamed me for what happened." I fell back into those memories—Ian's concern and his mother and sister tending to my personal needs after Augustus Templeton tried to kill me.

"I am indebted to the McClain family, as well," Bartholomew said. "I may never have found you again."

I smiled and touched his face. "And yet, we did find each other. Do you believe in fate?"

He considered the question before responding. "I don't know. There are times and events that seem preordained, but others seem entirely spontaneous."

"Our meeting again was fate. Events fell perfectly into place for us to become reacquainted and fall in love."

He gazed into the dying fire. "It's time I go home. I have court in the morning."

"Will you be here for supper before church?" I asked.

"Absolutely."

We stood.

He kissed me. "I'll see you tomorrow. Sweet dreams."

I sat in the library for another hour before going upstairs to bed. *What will the new year bring?* I wondered *Let's get through Christmas first.*

Chapter 62

24 December 1868

A letter in the morning post set my heart to beating rapidly. My hands shook as I ripped open the envelope with Mr. Green's return address in the upper left corner.

Miss Llewellyn:

I have spoken at length with the physicians at Philadelphia Hosptial about Mrs. Finch. Two of them are willing to testify to her sanity.

Therefore, I have again petitioned the court for a hearing on the matter.

The court has set the hearing for eight o'clock on 15 February 1869. I will once again subpoena you and Mrs. Davidson to testify.

Please set an appointment to speak with me upon your return to Philadelphia.

Best Regards,
Paul Green, Esq.

I tilted my head back and said, "Praise the Lord. Surely, Elizabeth will be released from that place this time." After noting the date in my diary, I stood and rang the bell to ask for tea.

Bartholomew arrived while I was upstairs dressing for supper and church. When I entered the library, he was standing in front of the fireplace, staring into the fire.

I glanced at the unlit Christmas tree, standing in the window, and raised my eyebrows at several brightly wrapped packages under it.

Without turning, Bartholomew said, "I see Santa has been here."

"I thought the household had to be asleep for him to come."

"Apparently, you just have to leave the room." He turned around. "You look beautiful, Priscilla."

"Thank you. Shall we go in to supper?"
He stepped to my side and offered his arm. "By all means."

Over supper, we discussed family traditions for opening gifts.

"Papa made me wait till after church on Christmas morning. We never went to Christmas Eve services. He did not like traveling River Road in the dark."

"We did the same. No gifts and no breakfast until after church on Christmas morning. Santa always wrapped his gifts and set them at our places at the table on Christmas."

"It seems odd to attend Christmas Eve services," I remarked. "But we live in town, so there is no logical reason to wait for tomorrow morning."

"When do you want to open presents to each other?" he asked.

"We are going to the late service, so it will be Christmas Day when we come out..." I allowed my thoughts to trail off.

"So, we could open them when we came back here," he finished my statement.

"Yes, if you do not think it too scandalous to be alone with me in the wee hours of the morning."

"I could bring you here and go home to sleep. We could have

a light breakfast and open gifts while my family is at church and then follow them back to Riverbend."

I ate while considering our options. "It has been a busy day. I prefer to sleep and open presents after breakfast."

Bartholomew let out a breath. "I was hoping that would be your choice. I spent nearly all day in court with a difficult client."

"I wish your mother had allowed Mrs. Reese to help with Christmas dinner. I hate to think of her slaving in the kitchen all morning."

"She cooked most of it today," he divulged. "She'll warm it after they get home from church."

"I never thought about actually cooking the meal. Interesting. Papa had a cook after Mama died. By the time I was old enough to assume those responsibilities, Mrs. Farnsworth had been with him for nearly twenty years. He would not hear of losing her, so I never learned to cook. I cannot even be trusted to boil water."

"Really? They don't even let you put on the kettle?"

"I once put on a kettle but didn't put any water in it. I had to replace the kettle and was banned from the kitchen."

He laughed. "I love you, Priscilla Cecilia Llewellyn."

I smiled and felt my face grow warm. "And I love you, Bartholomew Martin."

We sat in the library and shared funny and sad stories of past Christmases until it was time to go to church.

We used the buggy and rode through the quiet streets of Norwich to the First Congregational Church, where we took our places in the Martin family pew.

Candlelight shimmered in the sanctuary as families filled the pews. The congregation sang the songs of Advent, anticipating the birth of the child in Bethlehem more than eighteen centuries ago. The story of the child's birth was recited.

How frightened the mother of Jesus must have been. Yet, she gave birth to a boy child who grew up to save the world.

The final hymn was Joy to the World. We filed out of the church after midnight to falling snow.

Chapter 63

25 December 1868

Bartholomew arrived at my home shortly after eight o'clock.

"Shall we open our gifts before breaking our fast? I asked. Without waiting for a response, I grasped his hand and pulled him into the library, pushed him into one of the chairs that flanked the fireplace, and picked up my gift to him. "Open it."

He took the rigid present, placed it on his lap, and stared at the wrapping.

"Open it," I encouraged, lowering myself into the chair opposite his.

"Are you certain you don't want to open yours first?" he asked.

"Positive. Open it, please."

He untied the silk ribbon with a flourish and carefully folded back the red fabric wrapped around the wooden box. "Nice box. What am I to do with it?" he quipped as he worked the lid free and set it aside. "Oh, Priscilla," he whispered as he lifted the tanned leather case from its cocoon. He held it up and twisted his wrist to see all sides of it. He unfastened the clasp, opened the case, and peered inside. "What is this?" He held a small capped cylinder about eight inches long.

"It is called a fountain pen. They have been manufacturing them in Europe for about thirty years. A man in Canada made this one," I explained.

"I've read of them but have never seen one." He looked up. "Thank you. I shall use both daily."

"You are welcome."

He inspected his pen and case for several minutes before setting them aside and kneeling before me. "I have thought long and hard about what to give you." He reached into a pocket of his sack coat. "Priscilla Cecilia Llewellyn, will you do me the honor of marrying me?"

Tears sprang from my eyes, and I nodded, unable to speak.

He lifted my left hand and placed a ring on the appropriate finger.

I kept my gaze on his face. "Oh, Bartholomew," I murmured. "Are you certain?"

"I have never been so certain of anything in my life." He rose on his knees and kissed me." "Well? What's your answer?"

"Yes. Yes. Of course, I will marry you." I finally looked at the ring.

A single rectangular yellow topaz was canted slightly left in a gold setting. "Oh, Bart, it is beautiful." I kissed him.

He rose, pulled me out of the chair, and wrapped his arms around me. "I love you, Priscilla."

I started to speak, but he placed an index finger on my lips.

"I was contemplating this last night before I fell asleep. "I don't know when I started loving you, but I cannot think of a time that I did not."

"I fell in love with you when you first visited me in Philadelphia." I took a step back to look into his face. "I did not speak of it to anyone, but thoughts of you encroached at most inconvenient times."

We kissed again, and I held up my left hand to admire the ring. "It is lovely."

"The jeweler told me Topaz is the birthstone for November."

"I shall cherish it always." I snuggled into his chest, closed my eyes, and enjoyed being enveloped in his arms and breathing his scent.

He released me from his embrace. "May we break our fast

now? I'm starving,"

"Most assuredly, Mr. Martin." I placed my hand on his forearm as we left the library.

We served ourselves from the generous buffet laid out for us in the dining room.

I ate and stared at my ring. "Have you spoken with Mr. Brandt?"

"I spoke with him in August," he admitted. "He promised to keep the secret."

"That explains why Melissa never spoke of it. We should be married next summer."

"Agreed. You must fulfill your contract with the school. Where do you want to have the ceremony?"

"I have always dreamt of being married at First Congregational Church here in Norwich." I paused as I buttered a roll. "I may have to bring Elizabeth here in June. In that case, Agatha, and perhaps Beulah, will also come."

"I should think you would want your friends from Philadelphia here, regardless of how things turn out for Elizabeth." He looked up with concern writ on his face.

"I suppose." I rose and brought the teapot to the table. After pouring out a cup, I looked at him. "I ought to talk with Mr. Forsythe and Mr. Osborne before I return to Philadelphia."

"These decisions don't have to be made today. We shall enjoy the day, despite having to share you with my family."

"I shall make a list after we return from Riverbend," I announced. "Today is Christmas. Let us celebrate the birth of the Christ Child."

Wilson entered the dining room. "Kloth is waiting, ma'am. He and Yancy have taken the liberty of loading the gifts for the Martins in the carriage."

"Thank you, Wilson. We have eaten our fill and will be out

in a few minutes. Please convey our appreciation for the breakfast feast."

He nodded and backed out of the room.

Congregants mingled and called "Merry Christmas" to friends as we passed the First Congregational Church.

Kloth halted the horses on the route to River Road, waiting for the Martin's wagon to pass by.

A familiar buggy drove past, followed by two young men on horseback. It took a moment, but I soon realized Bartholomew's parents were using the buggy Papa had purchased for me. "There are your parents and brothers," I stated.

Bartholomew tapped on the roof of the carriage, and Kloth fell in line behind the riders.

It was a lovely ride to Riverbend. The sky was clear, and the newly fallen snow glistened under the bright sunshine.

There was a flurry of activity after everyone entered the dooryard at Riverbend. Mark and Joseph tied their horses to the corral fence and started to untack them.

Mr. Martin and Bartholomew began unhitching the horse harnessed to the buggy. Fenwick came out of the horse barn and spoke briefly with Kloth before assisting Mr. Martin.

Mrs. Martin took my arm and guided me towards the house. "Merry Christmas, Priscilla. She smiled at me.

"Merry Christmas, Mrs. Martin. It is a lovely day for a drive in the country."

"That it is. The snow and ice in the trees are so festive. No one could be cross or grumpy on a day like today."

When we were nearer to the house, she said, "Mark did a

poor job of clearing the steps. Do be careful, my dear."

"I shall."

"May I do anything to help you?" I asked as we entered the house and removed our capes, gloves, and hats.

"No, my dear. You are our guest." She touched my arm and directed me towards the family sitting room.

Bartholomew, Mark, and Joseph came through the door, burdened with the gifts we brought.

"Mercy, did you buy out the stores?" Mrs. Martin exclaimed.

"Bart and I may have gotten carried away. This is my first Christmas with your family." I looked at myself in the glass near the front door and replaced a few tendrils of hair that had escaped their pins. The sun glinted on the topaz in my ring.

"What is this?" Mrs. Martin asked, reaching for my left hand.

I smiled and leaned in conspiratorily. "Bart proposed marriage this morning."

"Oh, my dear, I am thrilled for both of you. It is a beautiful ring." She looked into my face. "I shan't say a word until he tells us."

We followed her sons into the family sitting room. The Christmas tree dominated the room.

"Papa and I always had our tree in this room." I turned to her. "Thank you for sending the decorations to me. It was most generous."

"Psh. It was the right thing to do. They're your memories, not ours."

Mr. Martin came in. "What aren't our memories?"

"Nothing to bother you with, dear. Priscilla and I are indulging in girl talk. Something I'm not able to do very often."

"Well, Mother, you will be able to indulge yourself in girl talk to your heart's content come summer," Bart said, standing beside me.

"Any, why would that be?" Mrs. Martin asked, managing to

look somewhat suspicious.

"Because you will have a second daughter-in-law sometime next summer," He announced. "Priscilla has agreed to become my wife."

His mother deserved an award. She appeared genuinely surprised by the news. She hugged and kissed me, then her son. "I'm so pleased for you both."

Mr. Martin kissed my cheek and congratulated Bart.

Mark and Joseph held back, appearing uncomfortable with the displays of affection.

"Dinner should be ready," Mrs. Martin announced after the excitement had subsided. She led us into the dining room. "Mark, Joe, a little help, please.

Mother and sons disappeared downstairs and reappeared carrying various platters and bowls filled with steaming hot food.

The meal was wonderful. I felt part of a family —a new sensation for me.

"I realize you've not had time to plan, but when do you expect to be married," Mrs. Martin asked.

"The spring term ends on 28 May. I can be ready to leave Philadelphia the first week in June.

"A friend of mine may require some attention. I'd like to be married at the end of June or early July."

"That will be a lovely time, my dear. It's a shame your father won't be here to walk you down the aisle."

"Now, Mother..." Bart began but didn't finish his thought.

"I know. I'm sorry, Priscilla."

"It is all right, Mrs. Martin. I do not know where he is or if he is still alive. He has never written to me." I realized it no longer hurt to speak those words. "I will ask Mr. Brandt to walk me down the aisle."

"Your father and Henry were always close. They met in school when they were six years old, and they've been friends ever since," Mr. Martin recalled.

There was an uncomfortable silence around the table.

"Let me help gather the dirty dishes," I said, rising from the table.

'Nonsense. We hired the last two orphan girls to cook and clean. They'll take care of all this," Mrs. Martin announced. "Shall we move to the sitting room and open gifts?"

Everyone pushed away from the table and moved to the family sitting room.

Bartholomew and I climbed into the carriage at twilight. Kloth had lit the carriage lamps to help light the way back to Norwich. Alone in the carriage, Bart said, "That went well."

"Yes, I believe everyone likes their gifts." I stifled a yawn and repositioned my crinoline.

"That's not what I meant. I wasn't certain how my father would take the news of our betrothal."

"Why would he have objected?"

"He's been known to be quite critical of your father. I was afraid he would make remarks about Ethan and Mr. Pennyman."

"I am certain many people are critical of Papa. It is all in the past."

"I know." He put his arm around my shoulders and squeezed. "I love you. Your past is just that—in the past."

"I love you."

We kept ourselves to ourselves for the remainder of the trip home.

Chapter 64

28 December 1868

As I sorted through the morning mail, I came across a letter with vaguely familiar handwriting. Upon inspecting the franking, I noted it was postmarked in New Orleans. I had nearly forgotten I had written to Jacob Smythe before leaving Norwich last August.

Dear Miss Llewellyn,

I'm sorry to have been so long answering your letter. We been at sea near six months. We came into port in New Orleans three days ago. I had no time to leave the ship until yesterday when I went to the post office for the ship's mail.

I'd gladly honor your request to bring your possessions to Norwich. The Emma *won't be going that far north until spring. I don't know where the* Evangeline *is at this moment. I asked Mr. Sudbroeker. He says she was going somewhere in the Pacific Ocean. I never been there, so I can't tell you how long she'll be getting there and back. The maps show it's real big and has a lot of islands in it.*

I'll write again after the snow and ice melt.

Your obedient servant,
Jacob Smythe, Purser

I sat back in the chair, allowing memories of my time on the Emma to wash over me. Despite my reluctance to travel by water, I was forced to do so and discovered I enjoyed being aboard a ship on the open sea as long as those trips were punctuated with periods of being on dry land.

Images of Ian McClain, with his windswept hair and striking good looks, played in my head. I was fond of the captain and his family but did not love him in the same way I loved Bartholomew.

I set the letter aside and shook myself out of the reverie that developed when I thought about Captain Ian McClain. I would write to Jacob to inform him I received his letter and understood the logistics of moving my furniture and other belongings. *He should be here about the same time I return to Norwich in the spring.*

I finished looking through the mail and went in search of a cup of tea.

Chapter 65

31 December 1868

Bartholomew and I looked forward to the annual New Year's Eve ball hosted by Rachel's parents, Amos and Sybil Downs. They had not hosted a ball since 1860.

As I stared at the invitation, memories of that last ball flooded my thoughts. *Before the grand march, Ethan took my dance card and wrote his name on the spaces for several dances. He escorted me through the grand march, and we danced the first dance. Over the course of the evening, he reappeared thrice more to dance with me. And we danced the last dance.*

I recalled his right hand resting lightly on the small of my back and my right hand atop his left as I waltzed myself around the library to the music in my head.

And then, it was midnight. The last strains of Auld Lang Syne still hung in the air when Ethan sought out my father to ask permission to court me, which Papa granted.

As exhausted as I was when I fell into the bed in one of the Down's guest rooms in the early morning hours of 1 January 1861, I thought I would never fall asleep. Yet, around noon, Mrs. Downs woke Rachel, Melissa, and me.

Over a meal that was both breakfast and dinner, the three of us chattered on and on about our dance partners. I could only talk about Ethan. Those other names on my dance card were forgotten.

I sighed and went to Aunt Marian's sitting room to talk with her.

Mrs. Imbert created a beautiful new ball gown for me. I had shoes made to match, and Norris took extra pains while dressing my hair and included one of the tiaras from Mr. Osborne's safe.

I could not explain why I was so nervous about attending this ball. I had not visited friends during the week, so no one knew about my betrothal. I fantasized about sharing the news with Melissa and Rachel.

When Bartholomew arrived, I was already in the library. Peanut lay stretched out her full length on the hearth. She raised her head and watched carefully when the door opened.

Bartholomew gasped when he saw me. He strode to me and held my waist while he kissed me. "You're beautiful," he murmured in my ear. "Are you ready?"

"I am."

Norris was in the foyer to assist with my hooded cape.

Yancy held the door while Bartholomew held my hand to assist me into the carriage. With the door securely closed, Kloth called, "Walk on," to the horses, and we started towards Calamus, the farm three miles south of Riverbend.

When we arrived, Rachel and Melissa were in Rachel's old bed chamber. I went to see them and left my cloak in her room rather than allowing the hired staff to handle it.

Rachel was heavy with child but did not expect to be delivered of it for another month. She reclined on the divan while Melissa and I stood.

The subject of Christmas gifts arose. Rachel showed off the beautiful necklace embedded with rubies Fred had given her. Melissa pointed out the lovely opal earrings Quintin had presented to her.

The two of them stared at me with questioning expressions. I slowly removed the glove on my left hand to show off the yellow Topaz ring. Their reaction was well worth teasing with the glacial speed with which I removed the glove.

My closest friends admired the piece of jewelry quite calmly until I uttered the word betrothed. They squealed and clapped their hands, and Melissa danced around the rather large room.

I stood with Bartholomew in the foyer, waiting for the butler to announce, "Mr. Bartholomew Martin and Miss Priscilla Llewellyn."

"Priscilla, how wonderful of you to come," Mrs. Downs greeted me.

"It is lovely to be here again, Mrs. Downs. Do you remember Bartholomew Martin?" I replied.

"Yes, of course. You're Catherine's second son. Rachel told me you are courting our Priscilla."

"Good evening, Mrs. Downs." He looked questioningly at me.

I nodded.

"Priscilla and I are now betrothed," Bartholomew announced to Rachel's parents.

"How wonderful. Congratulations, Bartholomew." She grasped my hands. "And we always have best wishes for our dear girl. Do you plan to remain in Norwich?"

"I must return to Philadelphia but will return in June."

"Amos, did you hear Priscilla's news?"

"I was speaking with Edward Henderson," Rachel's father replied.

"Our Priscilla and Bartholomew Martin are betrothed," Mrs. Downs behaved as though I was her daughter.

"Well done. Well done. Your father would be pleased," Amos enthused.

"Thank you, sir," Bartholomew responded.

"I believe this is the first time I have been through the receiving line at this ball," I admitted.

"You and Melissa Brandt used to spend the day with Rachel and come down at midnight," Mrs. Downs recalled. "I wonder where my daughter is."

"We shall talk later," I answered, squeezing her hands before releasing them and moving with Bartholomew into the ballroom.

"I see a couple of fellows I'd like to greet." Bartholomew indicated a circle of men huddled together in a corner.

"Go ahead. I'll likely be with Melissa and Rachel. You can find me before the start of the Grand March." I watched as he wove around groups of people, waiting for the dancing to commence.

Melissa appeared by my side, startling me. "I must find Dr. Jamison," she said. Her face was stricken with worry or grief, and her voice conveyed an urgency.

"What's happened?" I asked.

"It's Rachel. I think the baby is coming." She did not look at me but continued scanning the guests to locate the physician.

I felt my stomach flop and clung to the back of a chair before joining her in the search for Stuart Jamison. Not readily locating him, I wrapped my fingers around Melissa's wrist and pulled her along as I walked to the orchestra conductor standing on the dais.

"Excuse me," I said loudly. "Do you know Dr. Stuart Jamison?"

The conductor glanced at us as he arranged his sheet music on the podium. "As a matter of fact, I am acquainted with the gentleman."

"He is urgently needed upstairs. Would you be so kind as to look around the room and tell us whether you see him?" I asked. He calmly turned and gazed at the mingling guests. "Yes. He's near that group of young men there on the left." He raised his arm to indicate the men Bartholomew had joined.

"Thank you." Leaving Melissa to find her way across the room, I struck out and was beside the doctor in seconds. "Dr. Jamison," I called out.

"Priscilla Llewellyn. You are a sight for sore eyes," he declared.

"Thank you, sir. It's Rachel. She's upstairs in her old room."

He gave me a curt nod, turned on his heel, and rushed from the room.

"You alert Mrs. and Mrs. Downs," Melissa directed. "I'll go with the doctor."

"Is Fred with her?" I asked.

"No, and I have no idea where he is." She turned and followed the doctor's path.

I first approached Bartholomew.

"Ah, here is my soon-to-be-bride," he exclaimed, reaching for my hand.

"Hello," I greeted his friends. "Excuse us, please. I must speak with Bartholomew privately."

"What is it? You look as though you've seen a ghost." He guided me to a secluded space behind a pillar.

"It's Rachel. It may be the baby. Melissa and Dr. Jamison are going to her now." I opened my reticule and extracted a handkerchief. "We must locate Fred Butler and speak with Mr. and Mrs. Downs." I dabbed my eyes.

He placed my hand on his arm and moved towards the receiving line. The bulter espied us and stepped forward.

Bartholomew spoke with him.

His eyes widened, and his jaw slacked but did not open.

Quickly composing himself, he stepped towards his employers and spoke with them between greeting guests.

I watched Mrs. Downs' face turn ashen. She excused herself and moved quickly toward the stairs. I followed her, leaving the search for Rachel's husband to Bartholomew.

Rachel lay still on her bed. Her hair was loose and framed her pale face, which was contorted with pain. Tears ran from her closed eyes to her ears.

"It won't be long now," Dr. Jamison reported.

"She told me the baby wasn't due until January or February," I said.

"Babies come when they're ready," the doctor explained.

"Where's Fred?" Rachel asked, her voice husky.

"Bartholomew is looking for him," I assured her. "I am certain he will be here as soon as he's located."

There was a knock on the door, and it opened slowly.

"Fred." I turned and moved towards him. "Rachel's asking for you."

"I need all of you to go downstairs. The maid and I can handle this," Dr. Jamison demanded. "Someone will come down after the baby is born."

We reluctantly followed Dr. Jamison's order and filed out of the room.

"I'm staying right here," Fred declared, sitting on the floor beside the closed door.

"We will check on you," I assured him as Mrs. Downs, Melissa, and I returned to the ball.

"Is everything all right?" Bartholomew asked when I rejoined him.

"I believe so. Rachel's baby will be born soon. Dr. Jamison is with her now. There is nothing anyone can do for her that is not being done. Let us enjoy the ball. I have been anticipating dancing with you since Christmas."

"You may decide to return the ring after the first dance." He smiled.

"I am certain you are a marvelous dancer," I replied.

"I wouldn't wager on that." Bartholomew's brother, Mark, quipped. "He has two left feet. We're all amazed he can walk without falling on his face."

"Very funny," Bartholomew nodded to the lady on Mark's arm.

The orchestra conductor tapped his baton on the podium. The guests quieted to listen to his instructions for the grand march.

Bartholomew and I took our place in the line, about fifteen couples behind Mr. and Mrs. Downs, who led the parade. Mark and his companion were directly behind us.

"Where's Joseph?" Batholomew asked, looking over his shoulder at his brother.

"Search me. He's twenty-one, and I'm no longer his keeper," Mark responded. "Mother and Father are right behind Mr. and Mrs. Downs."

The guests settled down and followed our hosts when the orchestra played the first strains of the march.

The grand march was followed by a reel and a polka before the orchestra transitioned to a waltz.

Bartholomew led me off the dance floor after the waltz. "I don't think I embarrassed myself too much."

"You dance wonderfully," I praised.

"Those dance lessons weren't a waste of money after all," Mr. Martin teased.

"The two of you dance beautifully together," Mrs. Martin enthused.

"Priscilla makes me look good," Bartholomew responded, then turned to me. "Would you like something to drink?"

"Yes, please," I answered.

Mrs. Martin turned to her husband.

"Yes, Cate, I know." He grimaced. "Come, Bart, let's get our womenfolk a cup of punch."

Mrs. Martin and I watched father and son work their way to the punch bowl.

"I heard about Rachel." There was genuine concern in Mrs. Martin's voice.

"Dr. Jamison is with her. Perhaps there will be an announcement when the baby is born."

"I'll visit her next week," Mrs. Martin vowed.

Bartholomew and I danced and talked with friends, family, and acquaintances. He introduced me to a few friends from school and men from his army regiment.

And, suddenly, it was ten minutes to twelve. The orchestra stopped playing, and wine was served to the guests. The conductors counted down the minutes,

Melissa and Quintin stood with their parents and siblings to my left, with Bartholomew and his family to my right.

Everyone joined the conductor in counting down the last ten seconds—and it was 1 January 1869.

Bartholomew embraced me, then turned and kissed his mother and shook his father's hand.

I shared New Year's greetings with the Martins and then turned to share the first minutes of the new year with the Brandt family.

As the revelry calmed, Mr. Downs announced supper was being served.

All the guests followed the butler to an adjoining room where a sumptuous buffet was laid.

"Would you mind if I went upstairs for a moment?" I asked Bartholomew.

"Not at all. I'll hang back and wait for you," He replied.

"Quintin, would you mind if I accompanied Priscilla?" Melissa asked. "The three of us have been together for almost every New Year since we were babies."

"Go," Quintin replied. "I know better than to try to keep you three apart."

"Thank you," Melissa and I said and set off to Rachel's room.

Melissa knocked softly before turning the knob and stepping inside. I followed and shut the door.

Rachel appeared to be sleeping. Fred sat in an overstuffed chair he had moved from beside the fireplace to beside the bed.

"How is she?" Melissa asked.

"Tired." Fred smiled. "The baby is well. They took her away with the promise to bring her back."

"It's a girl?" I asked.

He nodded. "She looks like Rachel."

"Was she born before midnight?" Melissa asked

"I don't know. I was just let in to see Rachel."

"Is there anything we can do for you?" I asked.

"Do you think Bart or Quintin could bring me some clothes? I will give them a key to our house." He glanced at Rachel, then returned his attention to us. "I'm going to stay with them until she can return to Norwich."

"Certainly. I am certain one of them will do that for you," I said.

"Do you want us to send up a tray? Everyone downstairs is eating," Melissa offered.

"Is it already past midnight?" he asked.

"Yes. It's about half past," Melissa reported, looking at

Rachel's alarm clock.

"Happy New Year," Fred said.

"This is a wonderful way to begin the new year," Melissa observed.

"Let us hope it is an omen for things to come," I said.

"Bart and Quintin will think we've abandoned them," Melissa said as she leaned over to kiss Rachel's forehead. "We'll come to say goodbye before we return to Norwich."

"Thank you," Fred said as we quietly left and retraced our steps to the buffet supper.

Bart saw me to my door at three o'clock. I locked the door and went upstairs to bed.

Chapter 66

4 January 1869
Philadelphia, Pennsylvania

With all that had transpired in Norwich, it was nice to fall back into my daily routines in Philadelphia.

After two weeks of absence from their studies, my students were more eager to learn than I expected, and we continued with lessons at a brisk pace.

My ring did not go unnoticed by students, faculty, or the ladies residing at Mrs. Peele's boardinghouse. When asked about it, I smiled coyly and admitted I was betrothed.

Mr. Green sent a message reminding us he wanted to meet with Agatha, Beulah, and me.

We compared schedules and agreed to set the appointment for 13 January at four o'clock.

Elizabeth had recovered sufficiently to be returned to the asylum. I yearned to speak with her but was unable to see her owing to the two feet of snow lying on the Ladies' Pleasure Grounds.

I wrote to Melissa and Rachel, recounting my journey back to Pennsylvania and Elizabeth's plight. I prayed Rachel and the baby had been allowed to return to their home in Norwich.

Chapter 67

13 January 1860
Law Office of Paul Green

"I have spoken with the doctors and nurses at Philadelphia Hospital. They are emphatic that Mrs. Finch does not suffer from female hysteria and are willing to testify on her behalf.

"I have filed a petition for a new hearing. It is set for 15 February, and I am confident we will prevail this time."

The three of us sat with wide eyes and slightly opened mouths. This was not the turn of events I was expecting.

"What about Oliver Finch?" I asked.

"The asylum has barred him from seeing Mrs. Finch. I attempted to visit with her a week ago but was prevented from doing so. They continue to honor the request that she not see anyone except her husband.

"I can report that Mrs. Finch is well and in good spirits," Beulah offered. "She misses spending time with Miss Llewellyn and Miss Bentley. And she is relieved she is safe from Mr. Finch."

"Is there anything we can do to convince the hospital that having visitors is in Elizabeth's best interest?"

Mr. Green shook his head. "Sadly, no. As long as she is married to Oliver Finch, he has the right to dictate who may visit her."

We contemplated the situation.

"Is there anything else?" Agatha asked.

"No. I believe that is all for now." Mr. Green rose from behind his desk. "Thank you, ladies, for coming. I will be in touch."

"Thank you, Mr. Green," Agatha said.

The three of us stood and filed out of the office.

On the street, Beulah hailed a cab, and we returned to the boardinghouse.

Chapter 68

15 February 1869
Philadelphia Courthouse

I was nervous and excited as I waited in the gallery for Elizabeth's case to be called. A different judge was presiding, and I wondered whether his wife was at home or in an asylum.

Mr. Green sat with other lawyers, waiting for their cases to be called.

There were few people in the gallery. I tried to guess which gentlemen were doctors ready to declare my friend sane.

Elizabeth's case was called. Irene Davidson accompanied her into the courtroom. Elizabeth sat next to Mr. Green. Mrs. Davidson sat directly behind them in the gallery.

When called to testify, I repeated the information I gave at the first hearing and returned to the gallery.

Mrs. Davidson was also called and spoke of Elizabeth as a model patient. Although her opinion had no weight with the court, she opined Elizabeth was as sane as the judge.

Finally, Mr. Green called Dr. Jeremiah Phillips to testify.

No one came forward.

He called the name again, with the same lack of response.

The bailiff left the courtroom and called the doctor's name in the hallway.

Dr. Phillips was not in the building.

With no medical testimony, the judge denied the petition.

Elizabeth returned to Pennsylvania Hospital for the Insane at Philadelphia.

I was outraged that a physician would condemn a woman to live out her life in such a place. I prayed he had good reason for not being in court.

After school, Agatha and I went to Mr. Green's office. He agreed to see us without an appointment.

"Why wasn't that doctor in court today?" Agatha demanded.

"I went directly from the courthouse to his office. He was with a dying patient. She was just six years old." Mr. Green shook his head. "He sent a message, but it was delivered to my office after I left for the courthouse, and there was no one to deliver it to me. I wish I had known. I could have had the hearing postponed."

"I am sorry for the girl's family," I said.

"What now?" Are you able to file another petition?" Agatha asked.

"I can file again in a few months," he replied.

"Thank you, Mr. Green." I stood and moved towards the door.

"Good day, Mr. Green," Agatha offered.

Outside, we stood on the boardwalk.

"Do you want a cab?" Agatha asked.

"No. I want to walk and think."

"What are you thinking about? There is nothing to be done until Mr. Green can file another petition."

"Yes, there is." I stopped walking and turned to stand in my friend's path. "We are going to get her out of that place the week after the school term ends."

She stared at me with disbelief writ on her face. "You're serious."

"Yes, I am. We have talked about doing it."

"I know, but I always thought our plans were hypothetical. I never expected to put them into action."

"We cannot allow Elizabeth to be at the mercy of Oliver Finch or any other man." I began walking again. "We are going to help her walk out of that place and never return."

Agatha hurried to catch up to me. "All right. How are we going to do it?"

"We must speak with Beulah and Irene Davidson."

Chapter 69

25 February 1869

Letters between Norwich and Philadelphia were exchanged nearly weekly as wedding preparations began in earnest.

I tried to include Bartholomew in the planning but soon abandoned the endeavor as his responses were tantamount to no responses at all. He spoke with Reverand Arms about having the banns read and reserved the church for the wedding.

Grace and Melissa Brandt, Rachel Butler, and Sybil Downs were indispensable.

I pondered the reasons Melissa and Quintin Ross had not yet married despite being betrothed before Bart and I were. *I shall have to ask her about this when I return to Norwich. It is not a conversation I wish to have in writing.*

Chapter 70

27 March 1869

March had been unseasonably warm, resulting in snowmelt. Agatha and I decided to take a chance and visit Elizabeth at the asylum.

We were hopeful when we saw patients on the Gentlemen's Pleasure Grounds as we passed through the hospital gates.

As we turned the corner into the Ladies' Pleasure Ground at the rear of the hospital, we were heartened to see several women basking in the sunshine.

We were moving towards a bench when Agatha saw our friends coming out of the building. "Look, there she is."

I raised an arm and waved to get their attention while we moved towards them.

"What a wonderful surprise," Elizabeth said when we were close.

"We took a chance you would want to be outside today," I explained. "You are looking well."

"I am well." Elizabeth replied. "I have missed our visits and am pleased the weather has been so mild."

"Good morning, Mrs. Davidson," Agatha greeted.

Irene Davidson dipped her head. "Ladies. It's always a pleasure to have you visit Mrs. Finch."

I raised my eyebrows and widened my eyes. "Are you no longer using the alias Oliver insisted upon?"

"No. Since two petitions were filed and heard, it was determined by the administration that the ruse was useless. Her hospital records have been amended to show Elizabeth Finch is the patient."

"That is a relief." I glanced around the park-like setting and focused on the tall fence near the laundry buildings.

"It is nice to be addressed by my given name," Elizabeth admitted. "Though the change confused some of the ladies on the ward."

"How are you keeping yourself amused?" Agatha asked.

"I'm sewing and reading. I have no more paper or ink, so writing and drawing are no longer possible," Elizabeth informed us.

"We can rectify that," I assured her. "We will send paper and ink with Beulah." I gently steered the others towards the laundry to look at the door in the brick wall on the southeast corner of the property.

Mrs. Davidson looked at her watch. "I'm sorry, Mrs. Finch. It's time we go back inside."

"Drat. Just as I was enjoying being outside," Elizabeth turned towards Agatha and me. "Please come again next week."

"You couldn't keep us away," Agatha replied. And she leaned in to give her a quick hug.

"Take care of yourself," I said. "Goodbye, Mrs. Davidson." I took her hand and pressed a message into it.

She worked to control her expression as she nodded. "We will see you soon."

"Well?" Agatha asked, watching Elizabeth and Mrs. Davidson return to the three-story building.

"I gave Mrs. Davidson our message." I turned away. "I would like to look at that door again."

Very few women remained outside as we made our way to the wall.

I tried the latch and found it unlocked. "I wonder whether

the lock is broken."

"Perhaps there is no lock," Agatha suggested as we slipped through the door to the street.

We returned to the streetcar stand and went to Mrs. Doyle's Tea Shop to wait for Irene Davidson.

Chapter 71

24 April 1869

Plans for Elizabeth's escape from the asylum progressed. It was time to include her in the scheme.

Agatha guided our stroll on the Ladies' Pleasure Grounds further away from the other patients before broaching the subject. "We have devised a plan," I began as we approached the vegetation separating the Ladies' and Gentlemen's Pleasure Grounds.

"What type of plan?" Elizabeth asked warily.

"To help you leave this place," Agatha explained. "It's clear the courts are never going to allow you to leave."

"I see," Elizabeth's face was set in concentration. "I have considered leaving of my own volition." She stepped away from us and appeared to be studying a flowerbed. "I could never think how to achieve it. When do you propose to do this?"

"Monday, the seventh of June," I announced.

"I do not want to know the plan until the Saturday before," she stated, still looking at the plants.

"Is there anything you wish to take with you from here?" I asked, slowly approaching her.

"Yes, but how..."

"Give them to Beulah, a little at a time. We'll pack a bag for you," Agatha explained.

Elizabeth walked towards the laundry, obviously deep in thought. "Will you continue to visit on Saturdays?"

"Of course," I assured her. "We want to give the appearance

everything is as it has been."

"Where will you...no. Never mind. I don't want to know...not yet." Elizabeth turned to Mrs. Davidson. "Are you taking part in this scheme?"

"Yes. I will also be leaving the hospital. It's time I went elsewhere," the attendant admitted.

"Goodness. I don't know what to say," Elizabeth turned towards the three of us and squared her shoulders. "All right. I will start giving small items to Beulah today. Mrs Davidson, I believe I'm ready to return to my room."

Mrs. Davidson nodded. "Very well."

"We will see you next week," I said as we watched them cross the grassy expanse to the hospital.

"We should purchase a carpetbag for her," Agatha announced.

She and I left the asylum and boarded the streetcar to return to the other side of the river.

Chapter 72

29 May 1869

I fell into the seat on the streetcar, emitted a heavy sigh, and closed my eyes.

"Are you well?" Agatha asked.

"I am fatigued." I opened my eyes and smoothed my skirt. "I have been preparing my students for their final exams, packing my personal possessions in my classroom while sorting and packing my things at the boardinghouse."

"I've also been preparing to travel," Agatha professed. "How are your wedding preparations?"

"I received a note from my dressmaker asking to come for a fitting as soon as I am in Norwich. Rachel sent out the invitations a week ago. Melissa is selecting the flowers. I approved the menu for the wedding breakfast yesterday, and Mrs. Brandt and Mrs. Martin are talking with my housekeeper about the reception." I paused. "I think that's everything."

"On top of all that, you're making the travel arrangements to take Elizabeth to Norwich," Agatha sympathized. "No wonder you're exhausted. You've taken on too much."

"I will be fine. I promise."

The streetcar stopped. Mr. Green glanced at us as he moved down the aisle and took a seat behind us.

We traveled the remainder of the trip without speaking. The three of us disembarked at the stand near the asylum.

Mr. Green tipped his hat. "Good morning, ladies."

I nodded curtly and mumbled, "Morning."

Agatha was more effusive. "Good morning, Mr. Green. Have you news for Elizabeth?"

We walked briskly onto the hospital grounds and past the imposing building.

"I know you're upset about the outcome of the last hearing. I was not pleased, either. But, Dr. Phillips had a valid reason for not appearing in court, and he promised it wouldn't happen this time. "

"So you have a hearing date?" Agatha asked.

"No. That's why I am here today."

"We won't delay you then," I said. "You may speak with her first."

"Thank you. I shouldn't be long."

We rounded the corner of the building and entered the Ladies' Pleasure Ground. It was a pleasant spring day, and more patients were outside than usual on a Saturday morning. Most wore the standard nightdress and dressing gown, though a dozen or more ladies wore day dresses.

"There they are," Elizabeth pointed for the benefit of Mr. Green.

He quickened his steps to meet with his client.

I recognized Mrs. Davidson before I realized she was standing with Elizabeth, who was wearing a badly faded dress that had been poorly patched. "Why is Elizabeth dressed like a pauper?" I wondered aloud.

"Perhaps her good dresses are in the laundry," Agatha suggested and stole a look at me. "Or, she has no other clothes."

Over the past three weeks, Beulah brought clothing to be placed in the carpetbag I purchased for Elizabeth.

As soon as Elizabeth saw Mr. Green, she searched for us and beckoned us to join them.

He glared at us. "Do you wish to include Miss Bentley and Miss Llewellyn in this conversation?"

"I have no secrets from them," Elizabeth replied and turned towards us.

"Very well. I am seeking your permission to file another petition. Dr. Philipps understands he must testify. I will issue a subpoena to assure his appearance. I'm also prepared to ask Dr. Asher to testify."

Agatha and I exchanged looks but said nothing.

"I'm not interested in filing a third petition," Elizabeth stated.

He looked down and cleared his throat. "I am sorry to hear that. Please contact me if you change your mind." He turned and moved across the lawn towards the hospital.

The four of us watched him until he disappeared around the corner of the hospital.

"Well, that was interesting," Mrs. Davidson said.

"I don't trust either of those doctors to be at a hearing," I uttered.

"Dr. Phillips is a good man and doctor," Elizabeth stated. "The doctors at Philadelphia Hospital are overworked. I may be willing to give him a second chance."

"I have lost faith in Mr. Green," I stated. "If you want yet another hearing, it's between you and Mr. Green."

Agatha glanced at Mrs. Davidson. "What is your opinion?"

"I would prefer a court determine Mrs. Finch is sane," the attendant opined. "But, I have little faith it will happen." She stopped walking and hung her head, remaining in that posture for some moments before lifting her face to ours. "Why not pursue both paths? Let Mr. Green file his petition while we proceed with our plan."

Agatha, Elizabeth, and I pondered the recommendation as

we resumed walking towards the laundry.

"I believe that may be the best course of action," Elizabeth conceded. "If the escape fails, there will still be the hearing."

"I wonder whether the hearing can proceed without Elizabeth in the courtroom?" Agatha mused.

"That would be a question for Mr. Green," Mrs. Daidson said.

"That seems a reasonable plan." Agatha conceded. "What do you want to do, Elizabeth?"

"I prefer a judge to hear it and prove Oliver wrong. But, I don't share Mr. Green's confidence that a judge will set me free," Elizabeth admitted. "I shall be prepared to walk away from here on the seventh of June."

"Are you certain?" I asked.

"Yes. I really like Dr. Phillips, and I know he is very busy. A subpoena will mean nothing to him if a patient requires him." She began walking towards the copse of trees that separated the Ladies' and Gentlemen's Pleasure Grounds.

"I never knew you to own such a worn dress," Agatha blurted.

Elizabeth laughed. "It lived in the bottom drawer of my wardrobe. I wore it for some of the messier chores on the farm."

"It fits very well," I said.

"Yes, I've lost so much weight; dresses I wore before the war fit again. I have a few more items to give Beulah. I've made it known I've been doing some spring cleaning and ridding myself of superfluous things." Elizbeth looked at the door in the wall near the laundry. "Has that door always been there?"

Agatha looked at her watch. "We should go. I have several errands."

We hugged Elizabeth and Mrs. Davidson, then trekked across the lawn to exit the hospital grounds.

"It's odd not using the door in the wall," I observed.

"We cannot let on we know it's unlocked."

"Where are we going next?"

"Home."

"You said you have errands."

"I did." Agatha smiled and continued walking to the streetcar stand.

The boardinghouse was tranquil when we arrived home.

"Go up and put your things in your room, Agatha said. "I'll ask about a pot of tea and meet you in the drawing room."

"Would you like me to take your hat and reticule up for you?"

"Thank you, no. I'll do it after I've asked for the tea."

I wondered why Agatha was getting the tea before she divested herself of her things, but I went to my room and deposited my hat, gloves, reticule, and shawl on the bed. Out of habit, I glanced at the looking glass, neatened my hair, and returned downstairs.

I thought it odd that the drawing room door was closed but presumed someone might be having a private conversation and hesitated before entering.

Agatha appeared at the top of the steps. "What's the matter?"

"Nothing I know about," I admitted. "I wonder why the door is closed."

"The windows are open. Perhaps a breeze caught it," Agatha suggested.

I opened the door and stepped inside.

Barbara Adams, Daphne Crane, Callah Sheftall, and ladies from school and church were inside and greeted me all at once.

I covered my mouth with my hands and felt tears slip down my cheeks. "What is this?"

"We thought to give you a proper send-off." Daphne Crane came forward, took my hand, and led me to an upholstered chair in front of the cold fireplace.

I was overwhelmed and rendered momentarily speechless.

"We know you're not leaving for another week, but we wanted to have one last afternoon with you," Daphne explained. "Mrs. Peele has prepared sandwiches," Beulah said, carrying a tray into the room and placing it on a table with other finger foods.

"Thank you, everyone, for being here. This is a lovely surprise. I am going to miss you all," I said through tears.

As each woman approached me to express best wishes and goodbyes, small conversations broke out around the room.

"I misjudged you," Miss Adams stated as she lowered herself onto a footstool near my chair. "I am sorry for that."

"Thank you," I replied, uncertain how to respond to this admission.

"Eugenia Young was my cousin. She was married to a man who chose to remain in the Union Army when war was declared. He forbade her from showing her Southern sympathies."

"She was quite bitter about it when we lived at the boardinghouse in Texas," I related. "She did not deserve to die the way she did. May she rest in peace."

"I hope she haunts Augustus till the day he dies," Miss Adams spat. "He is as guilty of killing her as the policeman who shot her."

I recoiled at the statement. "I am sorry for all the trouble your family has had." I placed a hand over hers. "I never wanted any of it."

"I know. Eugenia's daughter explained it to me."

"How is Samantha?" I asked.

"She's still in Corpus Christi. She married that young man from Mrs. Doyle's boardinghouse. He is working with his father at a hardware store, and they have two children."

"They were establishing that store when I was in Texas. I am glad she is happy."

"I am, as well." She rose from the stool. "I'm sorry for my behavior. You are a lovely young woman."

I felt my face grow warm. "Thank you."

The afternoon was filled with conversations, food, and refreshing beverages. After our guests had left, all the boarders helped Mrs. Peele restore order to the drawing room.

Chapter 73

5 June 1869
Pennsylvania Hospital for the Insane at Philadelphia

Agatha and I finished marking final exams Friday afternoon and turned in the grades to the administration office as we left the school.

"I have enjoyed teaching," I observed.

"The students have liked your classes," Agatha related. "I cannot tell you how often students have entered my classroom still speaking French."

"That is quite gratifying. Oh, this is our stop."

We disembarked the streetcar and walked to the hospital.

"I seem to have a case of nerves," Agatha said. "We are doing the right thing, aren't we?"

"Yes. I cannot imagine leaving Philadelphia with Elizabeth still in this dreadful place."

"I shall have to find other occupations for my Saturdays," Agatha quipped.

"That should not be terribly difficult for you," I said.

We rounded the corner of the hospital and entered the Ladies' Pleasure Grounds for the last time.

"I am happy I never had to see Elizabeth inside that hospital," I declared.

"Beulah's descriptions are quite bleak," Agatha agreed.

"There they are." I indicated as we quickly moved towards Elizabeth and Mrs. Davidson.

"I was beginning to think you weren't coming," Elizabeth

breathed.

I looked at my watch. "We are here the same time we usually are."

"I believe we're both anxious," Mrs. Davidson claimed.

"Tell me, what am I to do Monday morning?" Elizabeth commanded.

We walked the grounds, with Agatha on Elizabeth's right and me on her left, as we explained how she would quietly walk through the door in the wall by the laundry and away from this institution.

Elizabeth listened and looked towards the door in the wall and back to the three-story hospital. "Where will Mrs. Davidson be? She's always beside me when I walk outside."

"Never you mind about me," Irene Davidson interjected. "I won't be far away. I'll meet you at the train station."

Elizabeth stood still, taking in her surroundings. She took a deep breath. "I will be ready."

Agatha and I sighed with relief.

Chapter 74

7 June 1869

Agatha and I sat nervously in the hired carriage on Powelton Avenue, watching the door in the wall near the hospital's laundry.

Agatha glanced at her watch, then resumed staring at the door.

"What time is it?" I asked.

"A quarter past ten."

"The train to New York leaves at eleven. We still have time."

Suddenly, the door opened, and Elizabeth stepped over the threshold, shut the door, and purposely strode towards the carriage.

I opened the door and held out a hand to help her enter the conveyance.

As she grasped my hand, she looked to her right and flung herself into the carriage, hitting the roof in the process. She landed on the floor.

I lost my hold on the door, which banged against the side, then swung closed, and blessedly latched.

The carriage moved quickly, jostling Agatha and me.

"What's happening? Agatha shouted.

"A man..." Elizabeth said as she used her hands and arms to rise from the floor. "He saw me at the door." She raised her lower limbs to slide onto the seat facing the back of the conveyance, where there was a small window. "He's in a buggy..." She settled herself on the seat and raised her eyes to

297

look out. "He's following us."

Our driver turned onto Forty-first Street and gained speed.

We all fell on our sides as the coach turned right onto Spring Garden Street and slowed to match the speed of the heavy traffic moving towards the bridge over the Schuylkill River.

"There are three or four wagons and carriages between us," Elizabeth reported as we righted ourselves and attempted to straighten our clothing.

Agatha handed Elizabeth a small bundle. "I brought these for you."

Elizabeth unfolded the fabric to reveal a hat, a pair of gloves, and a reticule. "Thank you." She picked up the hat and settled it on her head. "Is it straight?"

Agatha reached over and moved the hat a bit. "There. Now it's right."

Elizabeth pulled out the hat pin and pierced the hat to secure it to her hair.

While she was pulling on the gloves, our carriage made a gentle right turn from the bridge onto Callowhill Street.

"We're nearly there," I said, turning to look out the window behind my head. "I hope we're a good distance from whoever was following us."

"Could it have been Oliver?" Agatha asked.

Elizabeth shook her head. "No, it wasn't my husband. The man on the street was taller and heavier. He was standing beside a buggy."

"Let one of us get out first," I instructed as the carriage came to a stop in front of the Reading Railroad Station.

As she disembarked the carriage, Elizabeth drew the fabric the hat and gloves had been wrapped in close to her body and lowered her head to conceal her face with the brim of her hat.

"Follow me," I commanded when Agatha stood on the street with us.

"Where are we going?" Elizabeth asked.

"New York," Agatha said as she moved her head to look at the people around us.

The platform was crowded, and we soon found ourselves amidst the people waiting to board the train.

I breathed a bit easier as we climbed the steps to a passenger car and found four vacant seats together. Agatha and I sat side-by-side while Elizabeth claimed one of the seats facing us and reserved the other for Mrs. Davidson.

"Where is Irene Davidson?" Elizabeth wondered.

"I thought we would see her on the platform." I glanced around the car.

"Was she with you this morning?" Agatha asked.

"Yes. She accompanied me outside. When she went inside the laundry to deliver a message, I slipped through the door in the wall," Elizabeth related.

"Perhaps she was delayed by your disappearance," I offered.

"And perhaps she left the hospital grounds by the same means her patient used," Mrs. Davidson offered as she settled into the vacant seat.

Elizabeth held her hands to her chest. "I'm so relieved to see you."

"I had a buggy waiting around the corner," Mrs. Davidson related. I had to wait for that other buggy to pass."

The train began to move, and we all smiled.

"Someone—a man—saw me and gave chase," Elizabeth related.

"Your driver is quite skilled," Mrs. Davidson said. "He did a fine job of blending into traffic. I lost track of which carriage was yours. So did your pursuer. He wasn't able to take the turns at the speeds to keep pace and fell further and further back."

"We're safe now," I confirmed as the train began to move.

I tried to read but found my mind wandering. Finally, I put away the book and closed my eyes, though I did not sleep.

In New York, we first located the platform from which we would travel to New Haven, Connecticut, and then decided to go to a nearby restaurant.

On the sidewalk, Mrs. Davidson announced, "This is where we part company." She turned to Elizabeth. "I'll pray you are able to resolve your legal problems. I have Priscilla's address in Norwich and will write to you when I'm settled in my new situation."

"Thank you for all you have done for me." Elizabeth hugged the older woman.

"It was a pleasure to know both of you," Mrs. Davidson said as she touched her cheek to ours.

"I am sorry you will not be traveling with us to Norwich," I said. "Thank you for caring for our friend."

"It was my pleasure. Best wishes to all of you." Mrs. Davidson walked across the street and disappeared in the crowded street.

The three of us located a restaurant and enjoyed a small repast.

Norwich, Connecticut

Kloth and Yancy were waiting for us when the train arrived in Norwich. I handed the baggage claim tickets to Yancy while Elizabeth and Agatha entered the carriage. I stepped inside and settled on the seat across from my friends.

Yancy and Kloth secured the trunks to the carriage and climbed onto the driver's seat. I heard Kloth call out, "Walk on," and we were on our way.

"How elegant to have a maroon carriage," Elizabeth quipped.

"It is lovely," I admitted. "My godmother wanted to be able to locate her carriage easily," I explained.

"Hmm," Elizabeth uttered. "Your godmother was wise. Most people have black carriages. This one definitely stands out. Perhaps I'll have my buggy repainted..."

"If you still have a buggy," Agatha speculated. "Oliver may have absconded with it."

"I hadn't considered that. I must write Mr. McConaughy and ask whether my horse and buggy are still at the livery stable."

The carriage pulled up to the front of my house.

"We are home," I announced and waited while Yancy opened the door and placed the step under it for us.

My house staff greeted us in the foyer. One of the maids showed Agatha and Elizabeth to their rooms. I followed them upstairs, turning down a different hallway to my room.

I began unfastening my dress as soon as I closed the door.

Norris arrived shortly afterward, with Peanut at her heels. "Welcome home, Miss Llewellyn."

Peanut jumped onto the bed and settled herself.

"It is good to be home," I replied. "The trunks should be brought up soon. I think I will wear the blue plaid dress." I stepped to the washstand, wet a cloth, and wiped my face and neck to remove the soot from the trains.

After donning a clean dress, I went downstairs to the library and looked through the mail. Seeing nothing that required my immediate attention, I called for Wilson.

"Has Mrs. Reese said what she is serving upstairs tonight?"

"Roast beef," he responded. "There will be a nice red wine as well."

"We will not be dressing for supper."

"Very well, Miss Llewellyn. I shall inform the staff."

Twenty minutes later, Agatha and Elizabeth entered the library. "This is an enormous house," Agatha blurted. "How do you know your way around it?"

I chuckled. "I've been coming here my whole life. Should I provide maps to find your way?"

"No. We now know our way to this room. I believe we'll be fine," Elizabeth said.

"Shall we go in to supper?" I asked, leading the way to the dining room.

Chapter 75

15 June 1869

It had been a busy week since we arrived in Norwich. Elizabeth met with Dr. Jamison and Mr. Osborne. A petition was filed, and a hearing date was set.

Mr. Osborne assured us the judge would be amenable, though we had doubts.

Elizabeth sent telegrams to Mr. Green and Mr. McConaughey, informing them of her whereabouts and that there would be a hearing in Connecticut to determine her mental state.

The three of us went for dress fittings with Mrs. Imbert, giving my friends a glimpse of my wedding dress.

Numerous afternoon callers welcomed me home and were curious to meet my guests.

Melissa, Rachel, Mrs. Martin, Mrs. Downs, and Mrs. Brandt came for luncheon to discuss the wedding.

The hearing to determine Elizabeth's sanity was held on the morning of the fifteenth.

At the judge's request, Elizabeth recounted how she came to become a patient at Pennsylvania Hospital for the Insane in Philadelphia, the two hearings that resulted in confirming the diagnosis of female hysteria, and her ultimate escape to Norwich.

Stuart Jamison, M.D. testified that, in his estimation, Elizabeth did not suffer from female hysteria or any other mental disorder.

The judge signed the order declaring Elizabeth sane and capable of rejoining society.

We returned to my house and gathered in the library.

"What will you do now that you're free?" I asked.

"I will remain in Norwich until after your wedding. Then, I will return to Philadelphia and engage Mr. Green to obtain a divorce."

"I don't think Mrs. Peele has rented Priscilla's room," Agatha said.

"I hadn't thought about where I would stay. I'll write Mrs. Peele this afternoon."

While talking, I glanced through the morning mail, picked out a letter, and tore open the envelope.

"Something interesting?" Elizabeth asked.

"It's from Beulah," I related and began to read aloud.

My friends,

I am pleased you all arrived safely in Norwich, and I wanted to inform you of events here.

There was quite a panic when Elizabeth and Mrs. Davidson went missing from the hospital. A search was immediately organized, and I was questioned for several hours but gave up nothing to incriminate myself or any of you.

Mr. Finch arrived on Tuesday, loaded for bear, and made unfounded threats to which no one paid attention. The search was called off Wednesday.

I have spoken with Mr. Green. He is distressed that

you so easily walked away from the hospital and understands why you were reluctant to file another petition for a hearing.

I have secured five days of leave and will travel to Norwich on the twenty-fourth to attend Priscilla's wedding. Please recommend a clean and inexpensive hotel.

I'm looking forward to all of us being together again.

Your friend,
Beulah Snodgrass

"Oh, I can't wait to see Beulah again," Agatha enthused.

"She has been a true friend," Elizabeth declared.

"I'll have a room prepared for her and send Kloth to meet her at the train station," I decided aloud.

"Oh, she'll love riding in your maroon carriage," Agatha said.

Mrs. Ingram knocked on the door and entered. "I beg your pardon. "There is a rather coarse-looking man at the back door. He says he has a delivery from New Orleans."

"If the man is Jacob Smythe, please have him brought to me," I instructed.

"Yes, ma'am. That is the name he gave."

"Have the furniture placed in the bed chamber next to mine. I will have to decide where I want it all placed."

Mrs. Ingram left and returned shortly with Jacob in tow.

I met him near the door. "Jacob, how wonderful to see you again," I said and gave him a quick hug.

"My, ain't this a grand home," he breathed. "I come as quick as I could. Captain Sudbroeker insisted we bring your furniture on the Emma. We ain't been this far north in many years."

"I shall be forever beholding to you and Captain Sudbroeker," I declared. "Ladies, this gentleman is Jacob Smythe, the purser on the Emma, the sailing ship that took me to Corpus Christi. Jacob, these ladies are my friends, Mrs. Finch and Miss Bentley."

"I'm pleased to know you ladies. Miss Llewellyn is an exceptional young woman."

There was a momentary awkward silence.

"I best get back to the ship," he said.

"Please give Captain Sudbroeker and the crew my best," I asked.

"I will be certain to do it, Miss." He turned and made his way back downstairs.

"So that's the famous Jacob Smythe," Agatha murmured. "He's shorter than I imagined."

"He saved my life, for which I shall be forever grateful," I said.

Chapter 76

Mr. Brandt and I waited in the narthex as Melissa, my maid of honor, started down the center aisle towards the alter where Reverend Arms, Bartholomew, and his brother, Mark, stood.

As my friend reached the fifth pew from the back, Mr. Brandt extended his left arm. "Are you ready?"

I nodded, laid my hand on his arm, and walked slowly toward my future.

ThE EnD

NOTE FROM THE AUTHOR

Thank you for taking the time to read *No Longer Alone*

Please consider taking a moment to leave a review and/or recommend this trilogy to a friend. It is gratifying to an author to know someone liked their book enough to recommend it to others.

ACKNOWLEDGMENTS

Writing is frequently described as a solitary activity. The truth is, that many people are involved in the process. This book would not have been written without the wonderful people in my life.

My husband, Roger, is a font of knowledge, providing information and support to my writing.

Irene Morse, Gloria Getman, Shirley A. Blair, Keller, and Grace Dalton provide valuable feedback.

The baristas at Starbucks at Demaree & Noble in Visalia, California provide me with tea, snacks, and a friendly, safe place to work while also encouraging and supporting my writing.

ABOUT JUDITH BIXBY BOLING

Judith Bixby Boling has been reading and writing most of her life. She utilizes her research and writing skills honed while working as a paralegal and then as a construction specifier.

Boling and her husband are members of an American Civil War reenacting group. Her interest in this era is reflected in her writing.

She lives with her husband in Central California.

**FOR MORE INFORMATION ABOUT
THE AUTHOR VISIT:**

judithbixbyboling.net

FOLLOW HER ON:

Facebook
Instagram
LinkedIn
X

OTHER BOOKS BY JUDITH BIXBY-BOLING

ALONE TRILOGY

Priscilla Alone
Together Alone

TALES FROM QUIMBY

Founding Quimby

ANTHOLOGY

Tulare-Kings Writers Present Tales from the Strip Mall